JUST FOR KIC

ISBN-13: 978-15336

ISBN-10: 1533668558

Published by Wendlewulf Productions 2016

PRINTING HISTORY
Geoff Boxell Edition published 1972
Gama Enterprises Edition published 1998
Wendlewulf Productions 2016

Dedication

To the Rev. Bill Shergold who cared when others didn't.

To my mother, who worried about me on motorcycles, but didn't stop or restrict me.

To all the lads I rode with. I knew few of you by name and mostly only by nickname, but you were my mates then, and remain so in my heart even now.

Foreword

Mods and Rockers in the 60s: Sex, Drugs, Rock and Roll and street battles - Right? Eeer, not quite; not as I remember them. Sex was something you had to careful about, I mean if you got a girl pregnant you married her, so, unless drunk, you only did it with someone you would be happy to spend the rest of your life with. Drugs belonged mainly to the very late 60s and the 70s. The Mods indulged to a degree, but for the Rockers adrenaline from hard riding a motorcycle was the drug, though God alone knows what strange substances lurked in the foul muck that came out of the tea urns of the transport cafes we inhabited. Rock and Roll was the music, sure, but for the Rockers it was 50s stuff with Merseybeat thrown in. The Mods shared the Merseybeat, but flavoured it with Rhythm and Blues. However, tastes varied, and several of my mates, were Traditional Jazz fans. There were also big band and classical music lovers amongst us. The Bank Holiday street battles did happen. Mostly they consisted of a lot of shouting and posturing with physical contact usually coming about by accident. My own crowd tried to time and plan jaunts that avoided potential trouble spots! Yes there was trouble, and yes they were dangerous and exciting times, but mostly they were just fun, and both Mods and Rockers a load of youngsters out to enjoy themselves.

This story is semi-auto biographical. The stories I tell are true, but when you compress five years of events (1964-69) into one year of story, distortions occur. If you think I have exaggerated our deeds, think again - if anything I have toned them down, as I don't want my family to really know what I got up to! Originally Foxy and I intended to use this tale as a framework for a longer story, but it was not to be.

Although we were known as Rockers to outsiders, amongst ourselves we were 'The Lads'. Of the Lads in 'Just for Kicks': I live in New Zealand, Lew, Cecil, Methanol Pete, and Totter still meet up at any opportunity that presents itself. Foxy died from an hereditary heart disease soon after receiving the draft of the story. Jesus has turned middle-class. Graham joined his dad in alcoholism and died as a result. Mooney suffered brain damage in a motorcycle crash. Recently Yvonne died of a heart attack. Goosey and Sandy got married and live in NZ, and yes, the new girlfriend and I married too. I also still ride motorcycles, often too fast, or so the local traffic cops claim!

I originally wrote this tale for the amusement of my mates in 1972 when the memories were still fresh. I still read it from time to time, especially when one of my three motorcycling sons is in trouble. It is then that I need to remind myself that when I was young I wasn't perfect, in fact life then was; 'Just for Kicks'.

GR Boxell
NEW ZEALAND

JUST FOR KICKS
(Mike Sarne)

If there's one thing that I like, it's a burn up on
A burn up with a bird up on my bike.
Now the M 1 ain't much fun, till you try and d(
A burn up on my bike that's what I like.
Just for kicks, I ride all through the night.
My bird hangs on in fright, when I do the ton for kicks.
When my bird decides to turn up, I'm off to have a burn up.
A burn up with a bird up on my bike.
When I pass a little scooter, I blast him with me hooter.
A burn up on my bike that's what I like.
 Just for kicks, I ride all through the night.
My bird hangs on in fright, when I do the ton for kicks.
We meet the other ton-up boys at Fred's Cafe every night.
We just pop in to see the birds and sometimes, have a bite.
We spend a couple of hours just a tuning our machines,
With our black leather jackets and our oily greasy jeans.
If there's one thing that I like, it's a burn up on my bike.
A burn up with a bird up on my bike.
Now the M 1 ain't much fun, till you try and do the ton.
A burn up on my bike that's what I like.
Just for kicks, I ride all through the night.
My bird hangs on in fright, when I do the ton for kicks.

©Mike Sarne

Chapter 1: SEARCHING

ɔad glistened and sparkled in the cold night air.
:d appraisingly at it and snorted, his breath hanging
A crowd of lads milled around wiping dew off of
justing helmets, or fiddling with the bikes. One by
one the machines were started up. Cecil gave his Ducati a hefty
boot on the kick-starter to produce a deep flat fart from the
Italian single. Graham pumped his Ariel Arrow like a foot-
pump and got the temperamental two stroke going in a cloud of
blue smoke and a tortured scream from the exhaust. GR on his
old pre-war Velo gave his pushers a signal and sat on the
machine while they did the work for him, his lack of weight
making this an easier way of starting the bike than trying to
force a reluctant kick starter down on the high compression
single. Slowly the other bikes were started and warmed up.

Several lads walked onto the Zebra Crossing and caused the
on-coming traffic to grind to a halt. The bikes filtered through
the lads and lined up across the road, the riders in their
equipment looking like Roman gladiators. The throttles were
blipped at an increasingly faster rate until the sound reached a
crescendo. Lew checked that all was ready then waved his
white scarf. The Chelsea Bridge Grand Prix was on.

The two Arrows of Graham and Big Ray screamed into the
lead leaving the others to fight their way through the two-
stroke fog. Quickly Moony, Ken and the Big Feller on their big
capacity twins overhauled them, the riders fighting to keep the
front wheels in contact with the road. But it was GR on his
long legged racing single who was in the lead as the bikes
reached the end of the half-mile straight and came to the large
sweeping round-a-bout. GR's luck was in as there was no
traffic; he clunked down two gears in quick succession and laid
the heavy bike over, pouring on the power. Suddenly GR's

bike developed a mind of its own and skipped around the curves in a large vicious snake. Pulling the twisting bike upright and ripping open the throttle brought the errant bike under control, but he was now going far too fast to make it round the round-a-bout, so GR headed her up a side road and out of the race. The big twins hit trouble as they entered the round-a-bout. Moony and the Big Feller managed to dive into a gap between two cars. Ken, who was following, just missed hitting the second car and had to slam on his brakes, sending the back wheel into a twitching fit as it locked. The other two twins, with the back-markers close behind, carved through the traffic, first laying hard right then twitching over to the left to leave the round-a-bout and return back up the straight to the bridge.

The traffic on the return trip was quite heavy and the skill of the riders as they hopped up the line of cars amazed and petrified the drivers. The Big Feller was now clearly in the lead, being up the Bridge every night gave him plenty of practice and he was now using it to the full. The snarl from the bike's megaphones as he hit the red line on the tachometer suddenly stopped, started again, and then stopped to be followed by a loud bang. Moony waved as he passed the stricken bike and motored on, leaving the others to fight over the minor places. Moony braced himself for the finish. His bike hit the metal expansion plate that joined road to bridge, and he slid back onto the pillion seat to keep his weight over the back wheel and the front wheel up whilst the machine was airborne. Now over halfway along the bridge, he slammed on the brakes and prayed. His prayers were answered, the lights were green and he could allow himself the luxury of overrunning the crossroads at the far end of the bridge.

Ken, Little Ray and Cecil quickly came alongside and they all turned and waited for Big Ray and Graham to appear. The sound from their illegal expansion boxes heralded their arrival even before the smoke did. The traffic lights changed to red. Big Ray's tyres squealed as he slid to a halt the correct side of the line. Graham dropped two gears, wound it on, and headed for a gap between the cars. By a fag paper he made it, slammed on his brakes to avoid a car coming from the other direction, and ripped open the throttle again to dive through a gap between it and the car following.

"Wot do yer do fer an encore then, Ugly?" Cecil tilted his head back to observe Gra out of the only part of his goggles that hadn't steamed up.

"Mmmmmmm, Mmmmmmm," replied Gra behind the thick woollen scarf over his mouth.

"And you!" rejoined the others as they turned their bikes round to return to the coffee stall on the Bridge.

"Bet the Big Feller's upset" Big Ray smirked as they pulled into the vacant spaces amongst the ranks of bikes lined up in front of the coffee stall.

Lew looked up from cleaning his nails with a penknife. "Hardly, he's been trying to find out how far he could take the motor ever since he bought it. Now he knows!"

Little Ray, looking anything but sympathetic, walked over to GR who was examining the rear of his bike.

"Wot's up GR? Bike trouble?"

"Oil all over the rear tyre, that's what started the tank slapper."

"Oh yer, course it did." Scoffer Fenwick looked up from the cup of hot tea he was using to de-frost his hands, "I supposed you will be telling me next that you were leading when it happened."

"Was too" said GR, awaiting the traditional reply.

"Oh yeh, oh yeh. We know, we know," the lads chorused back.

Scoffer returned to the attack, "I suppose you will be telling

7

me next that if that hadn't happened you'd have won."

"Might have too," replied the dejected GR.

"Oh yeh, oh yeh. We know, we know."

Scoffer looked around for a new victim. "Hey Graham filtered through any lights lately?"

"Don't disturb the lad, he's still shaking," said Big Ray as he pulled off his gloves and held his hands over the top of the bike's engine.

Gra pulled down the scarf from over his mouth "I'm only shaking from the cold," he asserted.

"Oh yeh, course you are. I suppose you'll be telling me next that it's 10 below freezing," Scoffer gave a shiver and tried to huddle himself deeper into the warmth of his leather jacket and it's underlying layers of thick woollen jumpers.

"Balls," said Graham.

"Don't tell me your problems," returned Scoffer, "and don't forget what it says in the Bible: 'If your right eye offends you, pluck it out'. No doubt the same goes for any other part of your anatomy. Mind, in this weather, I doubt if you would find 'em anyway."

"Is he always like that?" asked a lad who was a visitor to the Bridge.

"Some people collect stamps, some people climb mountains, Scoffer Fenwick scoffs," said Lew with a shrug that lost him a lot of the warm air from inside his jacket.

The Big Feller arrived pushing his BSA Lightening Clubman twin, oil seeping out from a crack in its crankcase: "It's gone in a big way." He breathed steam everywhere making it difficult for anyone to see his face.

"Ain't you the lucky one," someone called out.

"Yeh," a smile broke out on the Big Feller's Neolithic face," yeh, suppose I am."

"Give him something to do in the evenings," Lew massaged his hands in an attempt to revive their circulation. "At least he will be in a tepid garage, not like us frozen masochists up here on this ice block of a Bridge."

"It is cold, isn't it," said GR holding a still warm empty teacup to his mauve cheek. "I've been thinking."

Instant cries of, "Whoa, steady boy." and "Don't strain yerself," echoed rpund the coffee stall.

"Oh yeh, oh yeh. I suppose you will be telling me next that you do it with yer brain?" called out Scoffer.

"Yeh I do. I have got one you know."

"Oh yeh, oh yeh. We know, we know."

"Anyway as I was saying; I've seen this nice kaff near Morden where some of the lads hang out. Far enough from home to stop nasty stories reaching mummy and daddy, yet near enough for when it's wet."

"Just lead the way my man," said Cecil inviting GR to join the exploration party.

"Let us know how it looks," mumbled Lew between mouthfuls of steaming hot-dog.

"Right oh."

Four lads broke away from the crowd. GR looked for his pushers. They straddled their machines and started them. Amid a chorus of catcalls they rode off into the night.

The lights changed to red in plenty of time to allow the lads to coast up to them four abreast.

"Say GR," Cecil pulled down the silk scarf from over his mouth "Where's this kaff of yours?"

"Just afore Morden, opposite the toy factory."

"Ah, that place. Ar tis indeed, a terrible place is dot one," said Cecil in his worst Irish accent. "The'd whip yer balls off and sell 'em back to yer as kidneys on toast dey would. Oh yes. And der rats; they'd be as big as donkeys they'd be. They even put saddles on 'em and ride 'em"

The lights changed and the bikes pulled off sharply, each

going fast enough to show it's potential but not fast enough for it's rider to be accused of trying to turn an exploration ride into a race. The next set of lights was already red and a queue of cars had piled up in two rows behind them. Gra took the inside, GR the middle, leaving Cecil and Gurn to double up on the outside.

"Where do you suggest we go then?" GR yelled across the intervening car at Cecil.

"Glad you asked me, I suggest the Caprice. All the lads go there."

"All the lads?" enquired a disbelieving GR.

"All those quality lads wot work with me at that superior establishment called Eelight Motors. We'd be sure of a welcome."

"Lead on Mac Duff."

The lights changed to green and everyone dragged off. For the first three yards the cars and motorbikes were fairly evenly matched but rapidly the bikes drew ahead. The bikes strung out into single file with Cecil in the lead.

At Morden they rode through the shopping area and then along the dual carriageway. Four times they turned round at the big round-a-bout and rode back into Morden and up to the George pub before turning back again.

GR pulled up alongside Cecil, "Where is it?"

"Up yours too," came the reply.

GR pulled down his leather facemask and tried again. "Where is it?"

"Oh where is it. Now lets see my man. Where is it?" Cecil looked under the bike, stood up on the footrests and examined the saddle where his not inconsiderable rump had been. Finally he gave a shrug. "Don't know. I had it yesterday!"

GR used his faster machine to pull ahead and waved the scouting party into the curb. "Look Cecil. Do you or do you not know where this kaff is?"

Cecil put on a very imperial look and peered down his nose. "In the words of Sir Winston Churchill: 'No'."

"Right," said GR resuming control of the party. "Let's go to that kaff I've seen."

"Yeh, but the Caprice must be around here somewhere!" Cecil made the last attempt to remain in charge.

"Enough is enough," Gurn wiped a dewdrop off the end of his nose. "Let's go to this kaff of GR's."

"If we don't get somewhere warm soon," added Gra, "I'll be going the same way as me brass monkey."

"What and make all the mothers in the country happy?" asked Cecil.

"To the kaff!" insisted GR.

They parked their machines at the end of a row of gleaming and not so gleaming motorcycles and approached the transport cafe. The front looked like the rest of the row of terraced houses to which it belonged, only the steamed up glass door betrayed its assumed use. The peeling sign on the wall said 'George's Café'; the equally dilapidated sign over the door said 'Bernie's Café'.

"I wonder whose place this is?" asked Gurn in his soft West Country accent.

"Leo's," replied a lad opening the door. "If you're coming in, come in. It's bloody cold."

They entered. The interior was a delicate shade of beige with contrasting steam stains, fly wee, and bare plaster patches.

"Helmets on the table," shouted a voice.

They undid their helmets and placed them on a table already overflowing with decorated headgear.

Gra went over to the counter, "Er, four teas please."

The toffee coloured man behind the counter wiped the requisite number of cups on the bottom of his non-too-clean coat and filled them with a thick fluid that looked like oxtail soup. "One ada shilling".

"Wot no deposit on the cups? People round here must be honest."

Gra handed over the coins with one hand whilst the other fished in his thickly greased hair for a dog end, and found three.

"Evening," said a lad in leather jeans.

"Evening. Nice clean place you have here," GR survey the tea stains on the floor. "Really nice."

"It's warm and we're welcome here." The lad in leather jeans looked over at Leo, who scowled back. "Well tolerated really."

"It's warmer than on the Bridge," GR wiped a large drop of condensation off of his leather jacket.

"Bridge boys, eh? We go there ourselves in the summer. Come down the end and meet some of the others." The lads followed leather jeans down a passage through into a rear room with a pin-table jammed in it and then into what had once been the kitchen. The poor lighting helped to hide the fact that this part of the cafe was even more dilapidated than the front half. A group of lads were sitting on tables, chairs, and an old piano watching a game of table football.

"Evening."

"Evening."

"These lads are from the Bridge," leather jeans inclined his head towards the scouting party.

"Go there ourselves when its warmer."

Gra noticed two girls in the corner who were looking his way and giggling.

"'allow darlin', where you been all my life?"

"Piss off."

"Pleasant company," observed Gra as he turned his attention to the moth that was slowly drowning in his luke warm tea.

"The birds are tougher than the blokes," observed one of the lads at the football table. Unfortunately his lack of attention had cost his team a vital goal and he vanished under a heap of irate mates.

"I've got a woman mean as she can be!" announced Jerry Lee Lewis from the jukebox.

"I like the music."

"It's all right so long as you don't mind it being at least five years old."

"Wot d' yer ride then?" someone asked and the next hour was spent debating which and what was best in the world of motorcycles.

GR looked at his watch. Eleven o'clock.

"What time does this place close then?"

"Twelve. Unless we upset Leo. Then it's earlier."

The four Bridge boys headed for the helmet table. Gurn looked up from trying to extricate his headgear. "Reckon as we might as well hibernate here for the winter then?"

"Yeh." GR started to buckle up his advertising hoarding of a helmet when someone at the counter caught his eye. "Look who's here," he indicated a lamp-post with a mop of golden hair. "Totter Dean."

The lamp-post looked up "Hello GR. What are you doing in a dump like this?"

"Ditto."

"Well some of me old mates from the cycle club," he indicated two lads in the corner indulging in some vigorous horseplay, "like to tour the kaff's. Foxy here;" the shorter of the two stood up, placed two fingers under his nose, and gave a Nazi salute, " he's got a car. So when the bikes are being patched up we chip in with the old petrol money. Provided the car's going of course. Hey do you ever see any of the other attendees from Southfields School for the children of gentlefolk?"

"Yeh. Believe it or not underneath all this clothing is good old Gurn, the tame yokel." Gurn removed sufficient of his gear

13

to allow Totter to recognise him.

"And we are just off now to tell Lew and the others that we think we ought to move in here for the duration."

Totter scratched his nose "In that case I think Foxy, Jesus, and me will do likewise."

Chapter 2: STRANGE MOVIES

The rain rattled on the dirty windows of Bernie's Cafe. Lew drew a picture in the spilt tea on the table. "What are we doing Sunday then?"

"Go up Box Hill I suppose," Gurn said as he tried to drink his tea without steaming up his glasses.

"Not enough bikes. It's been a bad month."

"Oh yeh, corse it has," Scoffer looked up from the carving he was doing on one of the table tops, "I suppose you will be telling me next even your bike is off the road."

"We'll go to the pictures," Moonie managed to say between the kisses he was exchanging with his girlfriend Jacky.

"Not up the back row we ain't." GR surveyed the figure in front of him that was engrossed in writing DUCATI backward in the condensation on the window. "There's not enough birds and I ain't doubling up with Cecil."

Moonie managed to pull himself away from Jacky. "No, no, none of that stuff when we go to the pictures. Haven't you been to the pictures with the lads?"

"Can't say that I've had the pleasure."

"It's the experience of a life time. You could write an epic about, and no one would ever believe you."

"What's on anyway?"

"It don't matter so long as it's a horror film. Though we had better keep clear of the Granada for a while."

The lads queued up outside the Mayfair Cinema at Tooting.

The few bikes in running order were parked near the exit.

"You ain't the trouble makers that were chucked out of here a couple of weeks back?" The manager blocked the way to the ticket office, sweat already beading on his bald head.

"Nah, nah, we all look the same with our crash helmets off."

The manager let the lads pass, but looked nervous and wrung his hands.

"Were you?" GR asked Moonie.

"No. We left just before the police arrived." Moonie led the way to the sweet kiosk where the others soon joined them. "Don't forget to get yer salted peanuts GR."

"I prefer the plain ones with raisins myself," GR answered innocently.

"Yeh." Moonie gave a chuckle. "But these go further."

A skinny usherette took their tickets and showed them to their seats. The lads ignored her and tromped on down the aisle and across in front of the screen, the noise from their motorcycle boots drowning the music.

"ROCKER, ROCKER," voices shouted from the darkness.

"WEE OH, WEE OH," replied the lads from Bernie's.

"Up here Rockers."

The lads and their girls headed for the voices. Little Ray indicated to GR two rows of seats from where the dim lights reflected on leather, metal badges and studs.

"It always does to know where the other lads are."

Amid much banter and horseplay the lads settled themselves in, forming the third row of the Rocker Block.

"We don't want you Rockers in here getting us young motorcyclists a bad name," objected one of the lads in the second row, laughter in his voice.

"Us? We are young gentlemen we are."

"Mmm. Speak for yourself ducky," interposed Cecil in his best queer's voice

"Give us a kiss and shut up," said Gra.

15

The lads erupted into song, first just the Bernie's boys, then, as they caught the tune of the Eton Boating Song, all the others.

"My maiden name is Cecil."

Cecil got up and started to conduct them.

"I live in Leicester Square. I wear open toed sandals, and rosebuds in my hair."

A shower of peanuts flew at Cecil's head and the dexterity with which he avoided them amazed even him.

"For we're all queers together, we normally go in pairs."

Gra stood up and linked arms with Cecil.

"For we're all queers together, excuse us while we go upstairs."

They exited towards the toilets amidst a shower of peanuts.

"Hah har, takes yer 'and off me crutch lad," exclaimed Cecil as he closed one eye and hobbled back to his seat on one leg followed by a near hysterical Graham.

"I see what you mean about the peanuts," GR said to Moonie. "The roasted ones certainly do go further, especially when thrown over-arm."

"Who's this Cecil what's causing all this trouble then?" the manager stood at the end of the row, his sweaty face dancing with a nervous tick. "It was you, wasn't it!" he pointed at Cecil who was pretending to hide inside his leather jacket.

"Wot me?"

"You."

"Wot name was it you said?"

"Cecil."

"Ah, no," Cecil looked all boyish innocence. "My name is Brian and I can prove it." He held up a tatty Driving Licence. The manager squinted at it and just managed to make out the details. Cecil pulled it away before the manger had time to read the address. "That Cecil you was after has left for the loo with his boyfriend. You'll probably find them in there now, contemplating their navels."

The disbelieving manager left for the gentleman's toilets.

"Peeping Tom."

"Hurry up or you'll miss your turn in the line-up."

The manager glared at the lads, and left to console himself in his office with a bottle of gin.

The skinny usherette showed a group of Mods into the row in front of the lads. The Mod's fear of trouble being allayed by the mock fright of the lads in the foremost row and the fact that they couldn't see the other two rows of lads.

"Evening Kokenut. Come for a quiet evening at the pictures have you?"

The Mods turned. Their eyes by now accustomed to the dim light, they saw the dull glitter that emanated from the rows of lads. They went to move seats, but it was too late, the film was about to start.

As the curtains drew back and the film started, the lads settled down to watch, all except Scoffer who took out a spanner and a screw driver with which he then proceeded to undo the retaining bolts of the row of seats in front.

The vampire came towards its half-naked screaming female victim and bared its teeth.

"Oi mate. Do you use Dr. Wernet's plate powder to keep them things in?"

"I bet he didn't get them on the National Elf Service!"

"I did," Foxy withdrew his two false front teeth and towered over one of the girls, who obliged with a scream and then promptly ruined the effect by giggling.

"Shh!" urged a middle-aged man across the aisle.

A shower of peanuts flew in the general direction of the complainant. Someone near him retaliated with a few peanuts of their own, the aim was out and the peanuts hit the Mods in the row in front.

"You wait, you git," threatened the biggest of the Kokenuts.

His supporters yelled general abuse in support.

"You trouble makers," Foxy yelled at them.

Cries of "Call the Police" and "Throw them out" erupted from the lads followed by a shower of peanuts.

A semi-decomposed corpse had trapped the hero in a sealed crypt. It shuffled towards him whilst he tried frantically to find a way out.

"Do you know you've got B.O.?"

"Nah, it ain't that. 'E just ain't got the ring of confidence."

"The only ring that Dinah's got is the ring right round her arse," someone sang.

The others took up the refrain. "Dinah, Dinah, show us yer legs, show us yer legs."

"LAW!!!!"

The lads shut up and pretended to watch the film.

"Just as well we've got our plain clothes spies out," Foxy remarked to Jesus who had just taken over from Scoffer as chief seat dismantler.

The law came into the theatre and, seeing all was well, went out again to tell the manager he was imagining things again and to collect a few complementary tickets at the same time.

"I fancy an ice cream," said Jacky.

"I fancy you," replied Moonie, and they collapsed into a deep embrace.

"If you want to do that sort of thing you should go to a park or somewhere." Despite his words, Gra watched the couple with interest.

"You're only jealous," Moonie's voice was muffled by Jacky's neck.

"Don't change the subject," rejoined Gra.

"Talking of changing subjects; where's my ice cream?" complained Jacky, fighting her way clear of Moonie and trying to straighten her clothes.

"Ice cream, choc ices, pickled onions. Peee-nuts," cried

18

Cecil.

The lads from Bernie's elected two unwilling volunteers and gave them the necessary money or pledges. The other lads did likewise with their pressganged volunteers.

"There's nothing like a good ice cream when you're at the flicks," said Gra who had got out of going to get the supplies because nobody trusted him with their money.

"Everyone to their own taste," Moonie took a dive at Jacky.

The goodies arrived and were duly eaten in a very noisy fashion.

Two Mod girls walked past. One, a buxom wench, was wearing bell- bottom jeans that were far too tight for her. Her rump looked like two dogs having a fight in a sack.

"She's cheeky ain't she," Gra said to no-one in particular. "Oi, darlin'," he yelled. The girl turned, "Scoff scoff get 'em off."

The girl gave him two fingers and continued her wobble back to her seat.

"Tell me Graham," asked Jesus as he passed the tools on to Little Ray. "Have you ever given any thought to this approach of yours towards the fair sex?"

"I don't mind your approach Gra," Cecil put his hand on Graham's knee. "Ah, aaah. V.D. of the kneecap!" Cecil screamed as he held his infected hand at arm's length with his other hand. It developed a mind of its own and he had to fight with all his might to keep it from his throat. He slid screaming and gurgling off his seat and was only silenced when those either side of him put their boots into his guts.

"Ah gee mommy, what shall I do with the ice cream wrapper?" asked Foxy.

"Put it in the trash can Butch," replied Jesus in a corrupt American accent as he opened the hood of the ex-army parka worn by the Mod in front and dropped his choc ice wrapper in. The other lads took the cue and followed suit.

19

Dracula was being held across a grave whilst two brawny peasants tried to impale his heart with a wooden stake.

"I can see right up your trouser leg," exclaimed one of the girls.

"Do you want to look up my trouser leg?" invited Cecil.

"Doubt if there is anything to see anyway," she replied with a disdainful look.

"Yes there is, provided you have a powerful magnifying glass," confided Lew as he rolled a fag with his right hand and continued undoing the bolts that held the seat in front to the floor with his left.

Jesus put his feet on the shoulders of the Mod in front. There was uproar as the Mods made as much protest as their inferior numbers would allow. Foxy and Jesus ducked under the seats and tied a few bootlaces. A big Mod stood up to emphasise his case, then sat down on the choc ice someone had put on his seat.

Jesus looked disgusted. "Here we are, sharing our ice creams with them, and all they do is moan. There's no pleasing some people!"

The film ended and amidst much jostling, the lads all moved back a row. The Mods in the meantime had gone off in search of reinforcements.

"What time does the programme finish Miss?"

The big bosomed usherette bent down to answer her questioner, revealing a deep cleavage, which made him come over all hot and sweaty. A peanut dropped between her breasts.

"Oh" she stood up and gazed into the valley looking for the offending object.

"Do you want a hand luv?"

"I wouldn't like ter see a lady struggle."

"They're only foam padding anyway."

She looked up hurt "They're not!"

"Prove it."

"Scoff, scoff, get 'em off!"

It was too much and she stormed off to complain and display the damage to the Manager. The force of her firm steps made her breasts bounce and tremble.

GR, still hot and bothered, shuddered and cadged a rollup off of Gra. His hands trembled as he tried to manoeuvre the elusive couple of strands of baccy into the right place on the paper.

The lights dimmed and the Mods, with their reinforcements, filled the two rows in front of the lads, the hoods of their parkas showing dull from where they had been washed.

The film started and an ice cream tub landed amongst the lads followed by a hail of peanuts.

"I knew it," complained an irate Cecil. "They only buy those cheap scooters so that they have got the money that allows them to sit upstairs at the pictures."

A shower of peanuts hit the Mods in front and war broke out. Despite some telling return fire the Kokenut Air Force in the gallery was getting the upper hand.

"LAW!"

Panic.

The manager led the way, a malicious smile on his thin face.

"I know which ones were causing the trouble. I memorised the badges on their jackets." The Policeman he had confided this information to just nodded his head.

The lads removed their jackets, the Policeman insisted that they put them back on again. When the confusion finally subsided the offending badges gleamed from a different part of the theatre.

"They must have moved," the manager's facial tick did a waltz.

The Policeman bent forward and caught a whiff of the man's breath. "Can I have a word with you sir?" He strode off, holding the manager's arm.

Foxy addressed the chief Mod; "I think a truce is in order."

21

"Till the Law has gone," was the sneered reply.

GR passed the spanner and screwdriver back to Lew and then they both moved up to help fill the gaps left by the lads who had gone to site elsewhere in the cinema.

A giant squid was ripping apart the crew of a half-submerged ship.

"That reminds me," said Jacky. "Can we stop at the fish and chip shop on the way home?"

"Twas on the good ship Venus, by gad you should've seen us," a voice in the rear row chanted.

"The figurehead was a nude in bed, sucking a dead man's penis," echoed the others. As the song got going even the Mods condescended to join in.

A man staggered across the blood stained deck impaled by a broken spar, his life blood pumping through his fingers.

"Acid stomach?" enquired one of the lads. "You need Eno, the peace maker." Even some of the ordinary patrons sniggered.

"I wonder where Cecil has gone?" Lew mused as he passed the tools onto Big Ray. An answering shower of peanuts arched through the silver beam of the film and landed on the Mods. War broke out again.

The ice cream tubs from the gallery were beginning to tell slowly on the lads, so they gradually melted from the battle field and moved elsewhere.

"I don't fancy being the last one here," remarked Jesus to Scoffer as he returned the tools.

"I think it's about time we made a strategic withdrawal."

The film ended. The victorious Mods made to get up. Some used the row in front to pull themselves up from their seats. It fell backwards, and the Mods collapsed onto their own seats, which also fell backwards.

"You know, you can't beat forward planning," said Scoffer as he and the other lads marched out.

Chapter 3: WALKING BACK TO HAPPINESS

GR knocked on the door of the neat terraced house, "Can Vernon come out to play?"

The tubby little girl giggled and shook her mop of carrot coloured hair. "He's in the garage."

Two more carrot heads appeared. "Who's that?"

"GR after Vernon."

"He's in the garage."

"I wonder if he's in the garage?" pondered GR as he headed for the wooden lock-up across the road. He opened the double doors and peered in. "Tell me Mr. Vernon Walter Lewis-Lavender; how come all the other kids in your family have red hair and you ain't? Did they have a different milkman in those days?"

"What do you want?" Lew wiped the sweat from his forehead and left a black grease-mark in its stead.

"Coming out to play?"

"No."

"Playing with your Mechano set then?"

"Putting a new engine in the bike."

"Is this the third or fourth engine?"

"A combination of the second and third." Lew fell to tightening a nut, the spanner slipped; he swore softly.

"Are you sure you ain't coming out to play?"

"Piss off."

"See yer" GR left and headed for the house next door to Lew's. He knocked on the door. It opened and a bright-eyed urchin looked him up and down.

"Can Graham come out to play?"

The child moved out of the way, "'e's in ver front room wiv 'is mates."

GR stepped over the bits and pieces in the hall and forced

open the stiff door to the front room. Totter, Foxy, and Jesus were lounging on the dilapidated settee. Graham sat in an ancient armchair, his feet resting on the mantelpiece.

"Evening GR." Gra fished behind his ear for a fag. "Where's the bike?"

"Which one? The fifty's sold, the Velos' being repaired, and the new Honda hasn't arrived yet."

"You forgot the BMW, the Harley, the Rolls-Royce, and the Mercedes." Jesus popped yet another biscuit into his gapping mouth.

Totter stretched his lanky frame. "Where are we going tonight lads?"

"Well there's the kaff, or there's the kaff, and if you don't fancy that there's always the kaff." As he spoke Jesus sprayed the others in the room with biscuit crumbs.

"We ain't got enough transport. Even Gra's bike is off the road."

"It needs a new battery, and I don't get paid till Friday."

GR looked out the window at the oil stained machine; Graham's care and maintenance of his motorcycle was the local byword for neglect. "I'm surprised that's all it needs."

"Well we'll go by public transport; bus then underground. That's how we'll go." Foxy stood up to emphasise the point, but the attempt failed due to his lack of height.

"Why not!" Totter also stood up, his lanky height emphasising Foxy's lack of stature even more.

"You coming Gra?"

"Nah, just breathing heavy."

They left the room as untidily as they found it and trouped out the house onto the pavement.

A cyclist weaved up the road towards them. An ex-army greatcoat flowed behind the dishevelled rider who appeared to be examining his front wheel by leaning over the handlebars. The lads watched with fascination as he weaved an intricate

24

pattern all over the road. Finally the rider pulled into the curb in front of the lads, stopped, and majestically fell over.

Totter looked down at the rider. "Evening Mr. King."

A bewildered and bewhiskered face looked back up at him. The bloodshot eyes tried, unsuccessfully, to focus.

"Nice weather, eh Mr. King."

At last the eyes seemed to stop working independently of each other. The figure lifted a hand in recognition, found it too much effort, and dropped it to its side again. "Eh, aarh, arh eh arh." Cider fumes wafted over the lads with each word.

"Yes it is warm for the time of year. Still, can't hang around here chatting all day." Totter smiled at the prone figure, "I can see that you're a busy man."

"Mum. Dad's home," shouted Gra as he and the other lads headed for the bus stop.

GR ran his hand over his golden hair "Feel naked without me crash helmet."

"Who'd want ter see your ugly, naked, body?" exclaimed a newly arrived Cecil as he slid alongside GR in a shower of sparks.

"Do you think the walk will do your fat figure any good? You know, like removing twenty pounds of ugly fat without having to have your head removed Ces?"

"When you ride a machine as powerful as mine you need all the weight you can get to stop the excess wheel spin."

"By the way; where is it? Don't tell me you've broken its rubber band again."

"Hey Cecil," Jesus joined in the fun, "Don't you know you have to put spaghetti not petrol in those Itie machines?"

Cecil was about to enter into a spirited defence of his beloved, if highly-strung and temperamental bike, when a bus pulled into the stop and prevented any further discussion on the matter. They boarded and settled themselves on a bench seat.

A middle aged conductress waddled up.

"One and five halves to Tooting please Miss." Gra fished in his pocket for some change.

The conductress looked. All the lads stood on their knees, except Foxy who just stood. "You ain't coming that one with me my lad. You're going to pay for five and one half. And like it."

The lads got off their knees and protested, Foxy smirked. Gra handed over the money. "Do you know you've got lovely brown eyes?"

The conductress wiggled with embarrassment.

"I really go for wenches like you," persisted Gra. The conductress dropped the change she was handing over, and bent down to retrieve it getting more flustered all the time. "Such lovely legs too. You really turn me on. I could go for someone like you."

She quickly handed over the money and rushed up the stairs.

"Nice bird that." Gra pocketed the money after checking it.

"She's old enough to be your grandmother!" objected Jesus.

"Yeh, but she gave me three bob too much change!" Gra gave a horsy laugh that made everyone in the bus look round to see what was wrong.

"Time to bail out lads." Totter led the way to the platform, Gra and Cecil stood on the edge. "Red light. Green light. GO!" he gave them a shove and they landed on the pavement and slid along, sparks flying from the hobnails in their jackboots. "Red light. Green light. GO!" Jesus and Foxy left the bus in the same fashion. "Red light. Green light. GO!" GR jumped, slid, hit an uneven paving stone, and landed in a heap. "Wee oh, wee oh. Spastic!" The bus stopped and Totter got off. "You lot are mad. Fancy jumping off a bus while it is still moving!"

The lads weaved their way through the stationary traffic in the same careless way they did on their bikes, and entered the underground station. The warm air came up and hit them.

"One and five halves please."

The man handed over the tickets. The lads, still on their knees mounted the moving staircase facing backwards. The ticket inspector peered after them short-sightedly.

After getting on the wrong train twice, they finally boarded the right one and arrived at Morden. The train pulled in. The doors automatically opened and deposited the lads in a heap on the platform.

"Get your boot out of my ear Cecil."

"Take yer 'ands off me crutch! Hah haah!"

They finally sorted themselves out and headed for the exit.

Graham surveyed the down moving stairs. "I wonder if you can walk up them?"

"There's only one way to find out my man, try it." Cecil indicated for the others to go past him.

"Lead on Mc Duff."

"Wee oh, wee oh."

The lads, even Cecil, charged at the stairs. The first half was easy but their legs soon started to get tired and they found further progress difficult. By a stupendous effort GR made it to the last two steps. Gra pulled him back down by his belt, they both fell back onto the others and everyone ended up in a downward moving heap; all except Cecil. Being last sometimes has its advantages and this was one of them; he stepped over the others and pounded for the top. Foxy's hand came out of the heap and grabbed Cecil's ankle. Totter made the next break but had got no further when Jesus and GR pulled him back and threw him onto the others. Finally, after much elbowing and shoving Jesus made it, to be followed by GR who crawled off on his hands and knees.

Two ticket collectors stood at the top, watching and laughing.

"Goodness gracious me. What a thing to be watching!" remarked the Indian one.

"Mad, that's wot they are," replied his white companion as he flicked his dog-end to the floor and ground it out. "Mad. It won't do ver 'ealth no good at all."

The lads sat or lay around the top of the moving stairs getting their breath back. Someone eased Cecil back onto the down stairs again, and he was half way down before he realised what had happened.

The Indian came over "What wonderfully warm looking boots you are wearing. Just the thing I am thinking for this English weather we are having."

"Very warm they are, yes." Jesus handed over the tickets. "Show him yer sheepskin lined ones Cecil."

Cecil obliged as the other lads headed out of the station into the street.

"Where are you getting these wonderfully warm things?"

"Eelights." Cecil quickly followed the others.

The Indian made a note of the information he had been given and handed over the tickets to his companion.

His mate lit a fag with his free hand and glanced at the tickets. He coughed and spluttered "Ere, these are for one and five 'arfs!"

As the lads reached the top of the railway bridge three bikes hove in sight. The first bike passed in a deafening roar to be followed by the more subdued snarl of the other two, the white leg shields of the last machine betrayed it as a Police bike. The lights at the crossroads were red but the first two bikes carried on, the first turning right, the second left. The Policeman hesitated for a fatal second before deciding to follow the first bike, but it had already disappeared into the maze of side streets.

"Looks like Megga and Chris are having a bit of fun."

"I'll be glad when I've got a bike on the road again," said GR wistfully as he stood and watched Chris reappear from a side road.

Cecil shook the dewdrop from the end of his nose. "Come on

or we'll be frozen to the spot."

The lads broke into a trot and used the impetus gained from coming down the steep bridge to hurry them towards Bernie's. The big front window was steamed up. Big Ray stood by the door drawing patterns in the condensation with the fingers of one hand, his other hand was holding that of a girl. "Evening lads. This here is Sandy from the Caprice."

"Evening Sandy. What did you come down here for? Did more than five lads turn up at the Caprice and pack it out?"

"Bloody cheek."

Graham leant against the counter appraising the girl's rear. "Yes it is cheeky isn't it."

The floor shook and the windows rattled as the bike with megaphones roared past at a high rate of knots.

"Sounds like Megga's lost his shadow then."

"That's good." GR sat down on the table, the steam from his cup joining the thick fog that hung overhead. "The cops will want revenge and will blitz the place for at least a week."

"You ain't got a bike at the moment anyway, so why worry?" Jesus' smug smile came from the knowledge that he was the only one who had come via public transport out of sympathy for the others rather than from necessity.

"I'm in pieces, bits and pieces," sang the jukebox.

"Hey Graham, they are singing about your bike," Cecil shouted as he disappeared towards the never-ending game of table football held in the end room. Graham didn't hear, he was too busy chatting up an unattached female. The others settled themselves down at a table and took up their hobby of ashtray and table engraving.

The door opened and in came Teri, a blood soaked handkerchief bound across her knuckles. She sat down with the lads, her glowing cheeks matching her copper hair. "Buy us a cup of tea someone." The lads looked at each other, tossed a coin, and the loosing Totter left to buy the tea.

"Wot you been up to then darlin'," drawled Foxy as he stretched his leg out in an attempt to make contact with her foot. His leg was too short so he settled for putting his thumbs under his braces and stretching them out in an exhibition of his manliness; they gave a loud ping as they parted from his jeans and whizzed over his shoulders.

"Teaching two Mod birds their manners. That's what." She tossed back her flaming mane angrily.

"Blimey. Did you win though?"

The flash in her eyes told Foxy that not only had she won, he should not have even doubted it.

"Now we're for it. They can easily muster ten times our number, come down here, and wipe us out." Foxy hit the table with a karate chop, a move he regretted the moment shooting pains ran up his arm.

"Doubt it," Jesus sneered." Our reputation will stop them. We know we'd be wiped out, but they don't. Anyway Teri's little bit of fun and games tonight will make them think." He got down on his knees in an attitude of prayer. "If the birds are as tough as that, what are the blokes like? From the fury of the Rockers may the good Lord deliver us."

Cecil edged past. "Not tonight luv. I've got piles."

"See I've got me uses!" said Teri proudly.

"Nobody ever doubted that darlin'." Gra sat down on her lap, his effort with the other girl having floundered on the fact that his bike was off the road.

The evening lapsed into the usual cafe routine of jovial boredom punctuated with games of table football and singing dirty songs. Suddenly the door opened and in came Lew, accompanied by a gust of cold air. The look on his frozen face told that his humour had not improved.

"Didn't expect to see you here tonight." Foxy, with an exaggerated gesture, designed to make the others jealous, lit a tailor made cigarette and inhaled deeply.

30

Lew ran his tongue over his top lip as he watched. "Yeh, well, I got it back together and made it work; after a fashion."

"Goodness gracious, great balls of fire!" exclaimed Jerry Lee Lewis from the speaker of the jukebox.

"Give us a roll Gra. I don't get paid till tomorrow." Lew turned pleading eyes towards Graham, who was having only mediocre luck with Teri.

"I'll give you a roll anytime sweetie," chuckled Cecil as he elbowed his way past with two cups of steaming tea, packets of crisps poking out from the many pockets in his leather jacket.

Lew ignored him. "Go on Gra."

Graham examined a screwed up baccy packet. "I don't get paid till tomorrer either and this is all I've got. You can have a dog-end though, if you like." He ferreted in his carefully greased and combed hair and produced two equally greased samples. He offered them to Lew.

Lew took them, acquired a piece of silver paper from Foxy's cigarette packet, pealed the metal foil off, split the dog-ends, emptied the contents onto the paper, carefully rolled it into a cylinder, lit it, inhaled, and collapsed in a fit of coughing.

"Cough, cough. Get 'em off," said Totter sympathetically.

A red eyed Lew glared maliciously at him.

Foxy had just embarked on telling Lew a souped up version of Teri's escapade when Ken and his girl appeared from the end room, a stranger in tow "This here is Geoff."

The lads nodded in acknowledgement.

"This here is Geoff," Graham indicated GR and then commenced to introduce the others. When that was finished the newcomer went to the counter to purchase some tea. On the back of his leathers was a large gold painted G in a five-pointed star.

"Evening Big G," GR yelled at the lad. The stranger turned round, then smiled slow-wittedly.

"By the by," said Ken. "The kaff will probably close early

tonight. Leo isn't at all happy." He and his girl collected their helmets and left without saying anymore.

Before this titbit of news could be discussed Cecil appeared convulsed in hysterics. "You ought to see Leo's face." He gave way to uncontrolled laughter that took a huge effort to overcome. Eventually he managed to continue. "Scoffer has just beaten him at football. First time he has ever lost in living memory!"

The victorious Scoffer emerged from the passage and smirked at the others.

"The teas are on me," he whispered. He then went to the counter and paid for a cup for himself. "Oh well if you lot don't want a free cup of tea."

The lads protested that nothing would give them greater pleasure than to join him in a celebratory cuppa, but Scoffer shook his head. "Too late now, you should have spoken up when I offered."

An attractive girl with short hair went over to GR.

"Go down the road and get us a packet of fags. Leo has sold out of my brand." She held out the necessary coins.

"Sorry luv, no bike."

"I'll give you a lift mate."

GR turned to see a lad he didn't know facing him. Sandy came over and put her arm round the lad's shoulder. "This 'ere, GR, is my little bruvver Kenny." She gave the not so little lad a pinch on the cheek and smiled.

"Ok then." GR took the proffered coins and followed Kenny out to the bike park.

"Right GR, get in and hang on."

GR looked nervously at the dilapidated motorbike and sidecar in front of him. He swallowed hard and got into the rickety chair. The four-stroke single burst into life and exhaled a cloud of blue smoke that any two-stroke would have been proud of. The chain jumped as first gear was engaged and then pinged straight as the clutch was dropped and the outfit rocketed off. Kenny was round the corner before GR had a chance to lean out over the chair's wheel, so instead he cowered behind the broken windscreen as the outfit carved its erratic way through the dense traffic at a rate of speed it did not look capable of doing.

They had just turned right into the main road when Kenny yelled; "There's a machine wot sells 'em!" He threw the machine into a U-turn at a ridiculous rate of knots. The engine screamed as the rear wheel lifted clear of the ground. GR flung himself over the saddle to try and prevent the plot from turning turtle.

"Give us the money GR, I'll get 'em. Save you havin' ter get out."

GR lifted his head from the saddle and smiled weakly, he didn't think he would have made it anyway. Kenny got the fags, jumped back on the bike, and ripped open the throttle leaving a pall of burnt rubber behind him. The lights turned to green as they approached and Kenny slid the outfit round the left hander as GR balanced precariously over the chair wheel. The bike hit the frost covered metal studs that divided the road. Kenny wrestled with the handlebars to try and regain control, leaving GR to pray for the first time in some years. Suddenly the tyres bit on the tarmac the other side of the road and Kenny threw the plot into a power-slide, managing to straighten up in time to just miss the lorry that was bearing down on them. They hit the top of the railway bridge, the outfit took off and landed with a force that should have broken it apart. The weak brakes ensured that they overshot the cafe, so Kenny threw the bike into a U turn that was, if anything, faster than his previous effort. GR almost stuck his nose into the rear wheel in his effort to keep things stable. They turned into the side road by the cafe. Kenny lifted the chair wheel just to show off. He kept it in the air until he returned to his parking place. Big Ray and

Sandy were waiting at the curb and helped GR out of the chair, wobbly legged. With their assistance he made it back to the cafe.

The girl who had been the cause of the trouble looked up. "You look like you could do with a fag!"

GR took one, lit it, and inhaled.

"I've brought you a cup of 'ot sweet tea." Sandy smiled encouragement to the white faced GR. "I read somewhere that it's good for shock."

Meanwhile Kenny and Big G were discussing ways and means of making Kenny's bike go even faster.

"While you were gone GR," drawled Foxy putting his thumbs behind the lapels of his leather jacket, they promptly pulled off their press-studs. " While you were gone, the lads commissioned a grand expedition to explore the outer reaches of Upper British Box Hill this coming Sunday. We have even commissioned enough transport to accommodate the brave souls who are willing to venture their all on this historic trip. Even L.T.2 will be going, God willing."

At this last piece of information even GR found it in himself to join the cheers that broke out.

"Wots L.T.2?" asked Big G.

"Wots L.T.2? You don't know what L.T.2 is?" retorted Jesus.

"Nah I don't. Wot is it?"

"You don't know? All the lads know what L.T.2 is! It's Lad's Transporter Number 2, Foxy's car."

Big G still didn't seem to comprehend.

"Car, brrrm, brrrm," added Jesus helpfully.

The penny dropped and Big G nodded good-naturedly.

"Its ad a closing time. Coma on now. Movada out," chanted Leo as he shepherded the lads towards the door. They looked at the clock. 10 p.m., obviously he had taken his football defeat very much to heart.

"I've cadged us a lift home on the Dreadnought," said

Graham.

"Can you give us a lift home Lew?" asked GR. "I've had enough of sidecars for one night."

Lew looked sharply at GR, but nodded his assent all the same. They marched out to join the milling crowd of lads on the pavement outside.

Amongst a host of lesser machinery sat Dreadnought. The streetlights reflected off its big V twin engine and off the highly polished alloy sidecar nose. Foxy and Cecil sat on the two car seats in the nose. Graham, Jesus, and Totter sat on the bench seat behind. The proud owner started the machine, then he and his mate mounted up "All aboard the Skylark!"

"Will it go, with all of us aboard?" asked an incredulous Jesus.

"1938 was a very good year for side-valve Royal Enfields," confided the owner's mate. The owner made no comment, it seemed that he deemed it bad manners for mere mortals to doubt the ability of his precious machine. The three-wheeled bus moved sedately off.

Lew and GR pushed their bike up and down the cul-de-sac in an attempt to get it started. Eventually they were rewarded with a flat cough and a cloud of smoke as the ancient James came to life.

Their ride went well until the pair were almost home. Suddenly the old James gave a cough, a splutter, and then cut out. They drifted into the curb, GR jumped off while Lew looked into the petrol tank.

"It's run our of petrol. The bitch." He dismounted. "The effing bitch, its run out of petrol." Lew picked the bike up off the ground. "The bitch!"

Two bikes pulled into the curb and their riders look at the unfolding scene in amazement.

"The dirty bitch, it ran out of effing petrol." By superhuman effort Lew lifted the heavy machine into the air and threw it across the pavement, over a low wall, and into someone's front garden.

"Er, do you want a lift home Lew?" enquired Dinky Cyril, Gra's mate.

Lew didn't answer but just mounted up behind Cyril. GR mounted up behind the other lad and they rode off.

"I always thought Lew was a placid type," the rider yelled back at GR.

"He takes a while to warm up does Lew, but once he does lose his temper; watch out!"

The rider wove through the back streets and came out at the Earlsfield lights. They were red and the bike stopped. GR leaned forward and yelled in the direction of the rider's ear "You two coming up Box Hill on Sunday?"

"Where's the start?"

"Lew and Graham's place."

"Right."

The lights changed and the bikes rode off.

Chapter 4: CATCH US IF YOU CAN

Mrs. Lewis-Lavender gazed out of the window at the crowd of motorcyclist outside. "I thought the lads would have been off by now."

Her husband joined her and snorted "I wish they'd hurry up and go. They give the neighbours a bad impression."

"But they are such nice boys. We've know some of them since Vernon went to Senior School."

"He'll only get into trouble going around with that lot, a scruffy load of troublemakers. That's all they are, going around creating a disturbance, causing trouble. I didn't get up to the things they do."

"But they are such nice boys, when you get to know them."

Outside, GR was teasing Totter about the state of Totter's oil

covered BSA Bantam, whilst Totter admired the heraldry on
GR's helmet. They saw Lew's mum watching them. They
smiled and waved to her.

"I think she likes us GR."

"I don't think his dad does though."

"Probably jealous."

"Probably is. When he was our age they stuck him in the
RAF and sent him off to be killed."

"All aboard, all aboard!" Foxy stood by the door of L.T.2 and
collected fares from his passengers as they boarded.

The lads mounted up, GR got on a little 125 Honda Benely
Sports behind Jesus. The electric starter whirled for several
seconds before the motor fired. The bike shook with high
frequency vibrations as Jesus blipped the throttle to warm her
up. For a pillion rider to get an erection was considered the
height of bad manners. GR wriggled with embarrassment and
exercised his full will power in an effort to curb the effect the
vibrations were having on him. It was an uneven battle and he
had to give it up.

"The vibes get to yer, don't they!" leered Jesus, highly
amused.

"Blimey," GR winced as Jesus blipped the throttle once
more, just for fun.

"Now you know why these bikes are sold as sex symbols."

The tacho hit ten thou as they seared off after L.T.2 and its
escort of bikes.

At the first set of lights all twelve bikes lined up together.
Totter on his old faded Bantam looked out of place amongst
the 'go faster' machines of the others.

"Last one up the Hill pays for the teas," Totter yelled at the
top of his voice.

"You can't afford it Totter," someone in the first rank yelled
back.

The lights changed and they roared off. The heavy traffic

slowed down progress but, even so, the others soon left Totter behind. The second sets of lights were already red and the lads had to weave and wriggle to get to the front of the stationary cars. Suddenly a flat exhaust note caught the lads' ears and they turned to see Totter riding along the pavement.

"Morning lads. See you up the Hill." Totter dropped the bike down the curb the other side of the lights and rode off.

The lights changed and the lads dragged off in an attempt to frustrate the cars who were making a determined effort to exterminate anyone who was a bit slow off the mark. The bikes soon caught sight of Totter and pounded past. Once they had passed he turned his old machine down a side road.

They were having no luck with the lights today and took the opportunity of the next enforced halt to moan about it. Totter appeared from the road on the right and swung in front of them, throwing his bike side to side just to show off.

Once they got onto the faster roads they started to get split up. Megga, Chris and the other big bikes had long passed out of sight when the four Arrows of Gra, Cyril, Doug, and Big Ray reached The Ace of Spades underpass. They screamed down the underpass, the high pitched whine from their un-silenced expansion boxes echoing and re-echoing off the walls. They emerged the other end four abreast streaming thick smoke. The cars following closed their windows and turned on their headlights. L.T.2 and the slower bikes turned off before the underpass and took the less popular, but shorter route. The roads on this route were too tortuous for high speed, but these vehicles hadn't got that anyway.

Megga and Chris easily held the lead at first but the deceptive bends on the Dorking Bypass allowed the better handling lightweights to catch up with the pack. The leader braked hard to turn off up the narrow twisting road to the top of Box Hill. Gurn had ridden hard, and it was him, Chris, and Megga who led the lads as they all swooped round the tight bends, hoping that nothing was coming the other way. Just as they entered the last bend Gurn hit the gravel on the side of the road; the back end broke away and tried to kiss the front wheel. Gurn stepped off the sliding machine, his only view being that of sparks being flung at him by the errant motorcycle. Chris and Megga didn't stop, the slower machines would soon be up, and they could see to the fallen rider. The race was nearing its climax with the cafe at the top of the Hill was in sight. Chris managed to pull a bit more from his bike and nosed ahead to be first across the line. He sat up, his face a picture of happiness, flushed with victory. It was then that he saw Totter sitting on a fallen tree in the car park drinking a cup of tea.

"About time you lot got here. This is my second cup!"

The shock of seeing that fair headed beanpole was too much for the two lads and they rode through the car park in silence to park their expensive racers next to Totter's oil dripping Bantam.

"Manufacturers may argue about revs versus c.c., but there is obviously no substitute for insanity," Chris muttered into his leather facemask.

Gurn on his now bent Triumph limped in, accompanied by the rest of the pack.

"How's the bike Gurn?"

Gurn took off his Buddy Holly glasses and wiped them clean. "Rideable." The shock of the crash had made him lapse into a heavier than usual Cornish accent. "Don't ask I how I be though."

"You'll heal, the bike won't."

The truth, or the near truth, of the statement prevented Gurn from replying, so he fell into looking at the damage he had sustained on the heavy PVC jacket he habitually wore instead of the more traditional leathers.

Gra took a couple of strands of baccy and rolled a fag the thickness of a matchstick. "I wonder where L.T.2 and the other lads are?"

The bikes cruised along the smooth road at a steady, unhurried gait. The pillion riders were playing cowboys and Indians with the passengers of L.T.2 . GR had just shot two of them when Mick, who was in the lead gave the signal to slow down. They bunched up.

"Wots up?"

Long-time Bernie's resident, Mick, leaned back and yelled as loud as he could so that the lads could hear through their crash helmets "Mods. 'undreds of 'em."

The lads caught the glitter through the trees as the sun reflected off of the multitude of scooters parked by the Wimpey Bar around the bend. Mick dropped back to warn Foxy.

The Wimpey was packed and hundreds of Mods milled about on both sides of the narrow road. As the lads rode past someone threw a hamburger at Jesus. Jesus and GR ducked and the missile flew overhead into the crowd on the other side of the road. Jesus took his hands off of the handlebars, put them to his helmet and pulled a funny face. Several more objects followed, fortunately most missed the riders who were now hugging the tanks of their bikes and going flat out. A plastic cup, half full of tea, hit the windscreen of L.T.2 which had dropped a couple of hundred yards or so behind the fleeing bikes. The dense liquid spread over the screen blinding the driver. Foxy slammed on the brakes and glided gently to a halt.

CRUNCH

Foxy hit a be-chromed scooter full in the bubble and had half mounted it before L.T.2 came to rest.

"Blimey."

"Foxy, your car is perverted trying to mate with a scooter!"

"Never mind that. Foxy, Get the hell out of here before these Kokenuts kill us!"

40

Foxy took his passenger's advice and jammed the car into reverse and then first. L.T.2 went faster than she had gone for years, only just missing the members of the large crowd that was attempting to surround it.

A parka clad Mod contemplated the short figure in front of him resplendent in crew-cut, tennis shoes, bell bottom jeans, and a T-shirt with 'Mini Power' emblazoned on it. "That was one of your car blokes, that was."

"Nah, they was Rockers. I saw 'em."

"Rockers only ride bikes. You're only trying to put me on. It was one of you car Mods."

They started pushing each other about, soon the whole crowd was fighting.

The convoy continued their interrupted journey along the winding roads until they at last reached the cafe.

"Wee oh, wee oh."

Totter waved to show them a place to park amongst the trees.

"I see you made it Totter." Jesus has a surprised look on his face. "Last time I saw you you'd just ridden over a round-a-bout instead of round it."

Totter just shrugged and led the lads over to the cafe where the others were already engaged in the never ending round of drinking vile tea.

DEE DAH, DEE DAH, DEE DAH, DEE DAH

Several Police cars sped past, two detached themselves and pulled into the side of the road. The occupants scrambled out and, after much straightening of caps and pulling on of gloves, they headed nervously towards a couple of hundred lads within and without the cafe.

"Good Cuntsternoon afterble," said Cecil.

The lead Policeman eyed him up and down, "You lads ain't been causin' any trouble? 'ave yer?" His hand tightened on the truncheon hidden in his trouser pocket.

41

"Wot us?" The lads tried to look all innocent.

"There's a riot down the road at the Wimpey Bar and it would appear that you Rockers," he rolled the name around in his mouth, enjoyed the end result, and so repeated it: "you Rockers, started it."

"Trouble makers that lot. We don't get up to anything like that, we're law abiding. We don't go looking for trouble, do we lads." Foxy turned to the others, and the lads all dutifully shook their heads, some from side to side, others up and down.

"Well you might get it all the same, last we heard," the Policeman looked to his companions for confirmation, "last we heard, a whole crowd of your friends," he chuckled, "your friends, are on the way down here cross country like to say 'ello' to you all." The Policemen all looked nervously about them, uncomfortable in the presence of so much leather. The lads looked at each other and shrugged. "Course," continued the Policeman, "we will be here to protect you."

The lads looked at the Policemen, and then at each other.

Totter shrugged, "You know, I fancy a ride home via the Salt Box on Biggin Hill. It will make for a nice, healthy, ride."

The lads walked unhurriedly to their machines leaving the law to spread the good news to the others at the cafe.

It was dusk, and the crowd at the Salt Box flowed out of the building and over the surrounding bike park.

"Methinks we will carry on to the Nightingale. Funny it ain't usually so crowded as this." Cecil wiped a dew drop from his nose.

"Where's the Nightingale?" enquired Gra.

"Where's the Nightingale? Where's the Nightingale?" drawled Totter. "You don't know where the Nightingale is? All the lads know where the Nightingale is!"

"Course they do," interjected Scoffer. "I suppose you'll be telling me next that the Nightingale is a kaff?"

"Yeh it is."

"Oh yeh, oh yeh. We know, we know."

"By the way," Scoffer quietly asked Totter, "where is the Nightingale?"

"Don't know. Round here somewhere I suppose."

The intrepid explorers set off, the darkening road spread out before them. They had just given up hope of finding Eldorado when they rounded a corner and were hit by an explosion of light. 'The Nightingale'; resplendent in its peeling shocking pink primer and khaki paint. The lads parked their machines amongst the assortment of cars and bikes and entered.

"Teds!" Foxy stared in amazement. "Teds. I thought they had all died out."

"Old Teds never die, they just fade away to the Nightingale," said Doug knowingly.

"I should 'ave worn me brother-in-laws drape coat." Foxy sat down on a battered old coach seat sending up clouds of thick dust, oblivious to all but the mythical Teds.

Cecil went and joined the queue at the counter. "Two teas and two of your rotten pies please."

The counterhand flicked his fag ash into a waiting cup. "If yer don't like 'em, yer don't ,'ave ter buy 'em."

"Can I help it if I'm a masochist?" Cecil walked back to the other lads, being careful not to spill any of the tea least it burned a hole in his boots. "Here you are, ugly," he pushed a cup of tea and a pie over to Graham. "I owe you this."

"I didn't think you'd remember," said a grateful Graham.

Cecil just smiled and rapped his pie on the hobnails of his boot.

"Not only the cup of tea you owed me, but a pie as well!" Graham was taken aback by Cecil's generosity.

"Don't say another word my man. It's just the natural result of my generous disposition," Cecil said magnanimously as he studied the pie for any damage resulting from his boot rapping.

There was none, so he proceeded to dunk it in his steaming tea. Graham studied the warm pie and his gastric juices rumbled audible. "A dentist best friend," whispered Cecil to GR.

"What was that?" enquired Gra, about to sink his teeth into the pie.

"I said I'd only buy one for a friend."

"Oh." Gra bit. There was a dull clunk, like stone on stone. "O O Oooooo H H Hhhhhh" Gra's bulging eyes indicated the pain he was in.

"Are a bit stale, ain't they." Cecil took out a large adjustable spanner from his jacket pocket and proceeded to pound his pie into edible fragments.

Big Ray was showing Sandy into a dark corner.

"I don't want much. I just want a little bit," the Undertakers sang from the jukebox.

"Scoff, scoff. Get 'em off," intoned Totter.

Sandy looked round, shocked. Big Ray also turned round, but he made a lecherous face at the lads. Sandy turned back to catch him before he could wipe the look off.

"Don't mind them." Big Ray assumed an almost innocent look, "I won't get up to anything I shouldn't."

Sandy nodded in agreement, but looked for an escape route all the same.

The lads fell to discussing the day's events, all except Foxy who was too busy watching the Teds, and taking in every detail of their dress.

A lad came over.

"Any of you lot play football? Only we are having the World Final, All Nations, Interdenominational, Lad Table Football Tournament in ten minutes."

Most of the lads indicated that they wanted to join in.

"How many are taking part?" enquired Scoffer, the Bernie's champion.

"Well me, and you lot at the moment, but I've only just

44

started to ask around."

Most of the lads left to start warming up for the championship.

"Shame about Bernie's closing," said the lad in leather jeans.

"Is it?" Even Foxy broke way from watching the Teds to listen.

"Yeh, Leo reckons that he's just loosing too much money, even with us big spenders down there every night blowing two bob a piece."

"Scoffer should never have beaten Leo at Football. I always knew no good would come of it." GR winced as he swallowed a mouthful of high-octane tea.

The lad who was organising the championship broke off recruiting participants and came over. "Where are you going to go now?"

"Back up the Bridge I suppose," suggested Cecil as he sprayed pie crust over all and sundry.

"Why don't you come up the Lombard on Clapham Common? It's still too cold to hang around the Bridge. You'll get piles sitting on those cold steel plates."

"Why not?" GR shrugged.

"Put the word round to the others. Those we don't see during the week we should see next Saturday when we go for our traditional ride in Richmond Park." Having given the order, Foxy went back to admiring the waistcoat of one of the Teds at the counter.

Chapter 5: YOU WERE MADE FOR ME

The lads pulled up in front of the little sweet shop. It was one of those bright days that give a hint of the spring that is just around the corner. Graham got off his bike and led the lads into the cramped shop.

The wispy man behind the counter looked up from his

newspaper. "Yes? Oh, its you. I suppose you want my daughter?" He looked suspiciously at the lads and made a mental note of everything that was on the counter before he opened the door to the room behind the counter. An attractive girl came out followed by a younger, and better developed edition. Behind her a tubby girl with bright ginger hair and a mass of freckles slyly slipped out to see what was happening.

"Hello Graham."

For once Graham was tongue-tied. He did however turn to the others with a 'How's about that there then' look as he led them all outside.

"This is my younger sister Eileen, and this is her friend."

Ginger took a fancy to Cecil. Cecil tried, unsuccessfully, to avoid her gaze.

"Does your sister, and her friend, want to come out for a ride then?" Gra asked the attractive girl.

The girl looked at him hypnotically. "Course."

Ginger had cornered Cecil against his bike. He turned his eyes to heaven and prayed. He received no reply, so submitted himself to his fate. "Suppose you want a lift Ginger?" His hopes for Divine help were finally dashed as the girl pulled down the pillion footrests and mounted the bike.

GR ran an appreciative eye over Eileen's generous figure, "Hello luv, want the ride of a lifetime?"

Eileen ran an appreciative eye over GR's gleaming and brand new Honda 305 Super Hawk. "Ok."

"Richmond Park, here we come." Gra adjusted his sunglasses, having problems with the process as they only had one arm.

"Wee oh, wee oh."

The lads moved off in their usual manner, demonstrating to the girls just how exciting, yet dangerous, life in their company could be.

GR placed his clutch hand on his passenger's knee and

shouted back into the slipstream. "Tell me, have you ever seem Ham Common? It's very pretty, particularly the woods."

The hunting season had arrived.

Chapter 6: GO NOW

Lads filled the small converted shop that was the Lombard Cafe and overflowed out onto the pavement. Bikes were parked on the shop frontage, in the curb, overflowing down the side alley, and even filled the courtyard of the lock-up garages behind the cafe, much to the annoyance of the tenants.

"Well, we've been here a few weeks now and I think it's a nice place, even if it is a bit small compared to Bernie's." Graham licked the paper of his ultra thin fag. Finding he had no matches he turned to Cecil, "Hey, Ces, give us a match."

"Your face and my arse."

Gra winced as he realised he had fallen for that ancient joke. Lew lent over and proffered Gra a light from a battered cigarette lighter. A smell reminiscent of hospitals invaded the small cafe. Gra lit his fag, inhaled, and came over giddy and faint. "Lew, what's in that thing?"

Lew shrugged, "Ether. It was all I could scrounge at work. It doesn't burn so well as alcohol, or even cellulose thinners, but it does, it does."

A slim pretty girl with long chestnut hair and a milky complication came over to the table. "You lads got any money?"

"Do I get value for my money?" Gra leered.

"You get a choice," she replied.

Gra smiled, put his arm around her waist, and pulled her down onto his lap.

"Get off you ape!"

Gra looked at her with mock surprise. "Why? I've got the yen." He rummaged in his pocket and produced his lucky

47

Japanese coin.

Someone started up the old song: "If I give you half a crown, will you get your knickers down?"

"I'm collecting for the jukebox, if you don't mind."

Gra put on a disappointed look, "Oh well, they say the best things in life are free," he joined with the others in making a contribution to the collection. "Just to console me in my sorrow," he said. "Put on the Strolling Rones." He wet his finger and drew mock tears on his cheeks.

Cecil fished in his pocket and produced a packet of French cigarettes he had treated himself to. "Got a match my man?" he asked Graham.

Gra saw his chance. "Your face and my arse!"

"If your arse is that beautiful," replied Cecil, "why do you keep it covered up?"

Gra admitted defeat and took to trying, unsuccessfully, to con a French fag from Cecil.

"I'm gonna tell you how it's gonna be," sang the Rolling Stones.

"You're gonna drop your draws for me. I'm gonna have it night and day," sang the lads.

"For love is love and not fade away. My love baby with the Cadillac," replied the Stones.

"You ought to see what we do in the back."

Mamma looked worriedly at her customers, she turned to GR who was leaning on the clean counter eating sugar cubes from the bowl. "Is thata really der words of that song? Is ita pop song?"

GR popped another cube into his mouth "More like a porn song really mamma."

"So I laid her on the ground," asserted Them from the jukebox.

"And slipped 'er 'alf a crown, said 'Get 'em down, babe, just get 'em down.'" The lads were now in full voice.

Mamma shook her head not fully comprehending. "I thinka you boys, you are naughty boys, that's whata I think."

Totter came up to GR and showed him a dirty, grease covered hand. GR nodded, put another sugar cube in his mouth and walked slowly over to Lew; "Tot Patrol," he whispered in Lew's ear. "Won't be long luv," he said loudly to Eileen who was looking daggers at Totter. Totter didn't notice, he was too busy trying to pick up the girl with the chestnut hair.

Lew and GR left the cafe, dragging a reluctant Totter with them. They just reached the curb as Foxy in L.T.2 pulled in. Everyone bundled aboard. Foxy addressed the other lads; "Just around the corner, two of them, haven't moved since we've been coming here." Foxy drove the car round the corner and into a dark car park. The lads got out and removed the inevitable locking pliers and adjustable spanners from the large pockets of their leather jackets. "This one first," whispered Foxy as they approached a partly dismantled Vauxhall of uncertain vintage. "I need a rear door, couple of spare wheels, and a front brake cylinder if you can make it."

They all fell to work.

"None of the tyres on this wagon are any good." Lew examined the wretched specimen in his hands. "Perhaps we'd better try the other one," Lew indicated a silhouette the other side of the car park.

The lads loaded the loot into the boot of L.T.2. and made their way over to the other car. They had just started to take off a front wheel when an irate voice screeched, "' ere, that's my car. Wot do yer fink yer doin'? 'elp, 'elp, Police. Someone git ver law."

Foxy led the others back to L.T.2 at a fast trot. Except Lew. Lew was a bit slow and the owner had collared him.

"'ere wot were yer doin' to me car then? Just you wait until the law get 'ere."

Foxy manoeuvred his car across the car park and came

alongside Lew at a fair pace.

Lew, by an acrobatic act he himself couldn't believe, jumped onto the running board. He then tried to get in through the window, hanging half in and half out. "I thought you said it was dumped?" he accused Foxy.

"Well it has been there for ages, and it looked a wreck, not like my limousine." Foxy patted the dashboard affectionately; the speedometer light went out.

Lew struggled in and, after causing Foxy to swerve across the road a few times, settled himself down on the front seat, being careful not to lose his virginity to the broken spring that poked up in the middle.

Lew looked round the tattered interior of L.T.2. "This is a limousine?' he asked sarcastically.

"Yep; it was quite luxurious in its day, and well in advance of its time."

"For example?"

"Free flow air conditioning."

"Oh." Lew was busy looking for the air vent when Totter, in the back seat, cleared his throat and spoke.

"Excuse me, Mr. Fox."

Foxy looked in the slowly revolving rear vision mirror to catch Totter's reflection "Yes, Mr. Dean, cur?"

"Never mind the air conditioning, close that bloody window. It's freezing in the back."

Lew tried to close the front window, but it wouldn't budge. "I suppose, Mr. Fox, that this is the free flow air conditioning?"

"Yep."

They arrived back at the Lombard to find the other lads singing Christmas carols.

"------six shiny tanners, f-i-v-e l-i-t-t-l-e b-o-y-s, four poxy cocks, three brown hatters, two fat turds, and a French letter in a pear tree."

"Where you been?" asked Cecil. GR showed him his dirty

hand. "Oh, Tot Patrol. Any luck?"

GR gave him a 'So, so.' nod, and made his way back to the counter and the sugar bowl, wiping his hands on his jeans as he went. He sat down and took hold of Eileen's hand. She didn't seem to notice; she was too busy giving Totter black looks. Totter carried on chatting up Viv of the chestnut hair.

Suddenly mamma made up her mind "That ada song youa boys were singing, thata song, it was a dirty song." Mamma was getting worked up "It's not a right that my little Luigi, and my little Maria shoulda have to listen to thata sort a thing." Luigi carried on admiring the motorbikes through the patch he had cleared in the condensation on the window. Maria carried on making eyes at one of the lads, and laughing at the words of the song he was singing at the top of his voice. "They are a good kids, gooda Catholics."

"What's being Catholic got to do with being good?"

"I'm a Catholic," said Graham.

"See what I mean!"

Mamma took no notice "It wasa alright till you lot came here."

"---- the rich girl rides in a limousine, the poor girl rides in a truck. The only ride that Dinah gets is when she's having a ----"

"Thats ada last straw. You boys, youra gonna go, and you ain'ta coming back!"

The North Clapham Night Riders Choral Society stopped in mid song.

"What?"

"Out!"

The ex-Bernie's, and now ex-Lombard, lads looked at each other, shrugged, collected their helmets, and left.

"All up the Bridge."

Eileen looked daggers at Totter as he helped Viv mount up on his battered Bantam.

51

The first away rode along the road at a sedate pace to allow the others to catch up. They spread across four lanes of the road and sat at the lights, waiting for them to change. When green came up no one dragged off, they all played cat and mouse; waiting for someone else to make the first move, but no one did. The second set of lights was also red when they came up, but changed to green as they arrived. Someone gave it 'Arse 'oles' so did the rest. Big Ray, on his newly acquired Matchless, was in front. Sandy on the pillion turned and poked her tongue out at the others. Two Arrows were close behind as they went round some tight bends, sparks trailing from their grounding centre-stands and exhaust systems. By the next straight the big bikes had caught up and were taking over.

Switching from main fuel tap to reserve cost GR quite a lot of time, and he was last in the pack as they came up to another set of lights. The bikes roared through on green, GR only just made it as the amber turned to red. The packed ranks of cars on the right and left of him poured on the gas and dragged off in an attempt to steam roller him. GR opened the Honda up, the tacho hit 10,000, the engine screamed in ecstasy and the footrests grounded as he laid it over in front of the charging cars. 12,000 and up into second. The front wheel pawed the air and the back end twitched. Eileen almost bent the grab bar as she hung on for grim death. Up into third, GR looked into his mirrors, the blurred images he saw told him that he was far enough ahead of the cars to ease off now. He came along side Ken who had watched him; "Bet you didn't think the old Tokyo war horse would go that fast Ken!" GR's eyes burned with excitement.

"Bet you didn't either," rejoined Ken. "Nor did they," he indicated the fast receding cars.

Ken's girlfriend gave Eileen a sympathetic smile, Eileen smiled back, then ducked her head inside her voluminous jacket to light a fag.

Lew had bought GR's old Velo and had put a sidecar chassis on it. He was just thinking that "…although it might go all right, engine wise, it was a foul handling camel," when a car pulled out of a side road right across his nose. Lew slammed on the brakes and slowed a fraction. He knew that he was too close and would not be able to avoid a collision. Almost without thinking, he threw the outfit sideways into a right-hand turn, slid the plot right across the road and down an alley. A fag paper was all you could have got between the outfit and the walls of the buildings on either side. Jesus jumped off the chassis and, with Lew's help, pulled the outfit back onto the road. Jesus leapt back on and just managed to sit down on the car seat attached to the chassis before Lew dragged off. Jesus slipped his hand through the fan belt strapped to the down tube of the sidecar attachment frame and prepared for action.

Lew caught up with the car and nipped in front of it. He gave the driver a V sign. The car moved up and touched the rear of the outfit. Lew turned into a side road on his left leaving the car to carry straight on. Lew then swerved the outfit back onto the main road and sat on the car's tail. The big Velo was getting into its stride as Lew pulled alongside the car and stared at the driver. The youngster leered back. Lew edged the outfit over until the wheel axle of the sidecar chassis touched the car, he then dropped down a cog and wound it on. As on most of the sidecars ridden by the lads, an additional nut had been wound onto the axle. Into the unused part of the thread was screwed a length of steel studding that extended the axle by six inches. The extension pierced the door sill of the car. As the motorcycle accelerated away the axle opened the car's sill like a can of beans. The car's driver gripped the steering wheel so tight his knuckles showed white and, a look of revenge on his face, closed up. Jesus turned round and waved his adjustable spanner at him, the car pulled back.

Jesus used the strap to pull himself up and spoke to Lew. "I always thought you were a quiet bloke Lew, meek even."

Lew just muttered and continued to fight his ill handling machine.

"Welcome home," said the Big Feller as the stragglers pulled into the vacant spaces on the Bridge.

"Want a cuppa tea?" GR guided Eileen towards the coffee stall in an attempt to stop her staring maliciously at Totter and Viv; it was getting to be an embarrassing habit.

"Two teas. That will be two bob," the man with the dirty apron behind the counter wiped his nose on the back of his hand and then held out the contaminated paw for the money.

"A shilling for a cup of tea? That's dear, that's a bit much," a look of genuine shock crossed Eileen's young face.

"Yeh, well, half of it is a returnable deposit," explained GR.

"Why do they put a deposit on the cups?" Eileen passed the chipped cup from hand to hand in order to prevent her fingers from getting burnt.

DA DAH, DE DA DAH DAH DAH DA sang an air-horn as a gaggle of scooters came along the Bridge and turned into Battersea Park. Half a dozen cups and plates followed them.

"Ask a silly question," said GR.

Two Police bikes hove in sight and the lads raced to their bikes. Those who could, turned on their parking lights, those that couldn't and those without road tax, rode off. The two all white motorcycles parked on the other side of the road. The two riders, in their outmoded dress, crossed and approached the lads, appraising both lads and machines as they came.

"Evening all."

"Evening," the lads replied apprehensively.

"Whose bike is this then?" one of the Policemen pointed to a gleaming machine with a gigantic alloy tank.

"Oh ---- er ---- mine," admitted a weedy looking lad.

"Not bad, not bad at all," mused the law as he and his

companion examined the machine. They both rubbed their hands together to get the circulation going again. "Tell me, how on earth did you manage to get that Vincent engine into that Norton frame without using a shoehorn?"

The owner brightened up and joined the law, entering into a discussion about the mechanics of the hybrid monster.

"I thought we were in trouble," whispered Viv as she nibbled Totter's ear.

"Most of 'em are all right, it's just a few that are nasty bastards." He pulled Viv closer, as much for the warmth as anything else.

"Blimey, look who's here!" Foxy indicated a motorcyclist who had just pulled in on a small 125cc Honda. The rider's nylon anorak and clean trousers set him apart from the rest of the Bridge's inhabitants. "Goosey, I thought you said that you'd never come out with a crowd of yobs and toughs like us?"

Goosey looked over and said, somewhat slowly, "Totter asked me to take her up to that cafe you go to," he indicated to a slight young girl engaged in an animated conversation with Eileen. "But when I got there, after twice getting lost, they said that you'd left for Chelsea Bridge. So I brought her here." Goosey looked round at the lads, when they didn't move in to eat him he relaxed and went to the stall to purchase a cup of tea.

"Who's he?" Gra asked.

"You've heard of sweet sixteen and never been kissed?" remarked Jesus, with an edge of scorn to his voice.

"Yeh."

"Well change the sixteen for twenty. He still thinks push bikes are the ultimate. I don't think he'll ever make a lad."

Gra moved over to inspect the push bike enthusiast.

Eileen and Goosey's pillion rider had their heads together. Eileen's brown mane contrasted with the golden hair of the other. The streetlights made the young girl's hair glisten, and reflected in the tears she was fighting to hold back. Eileen gave the occupied Totter another evil look and then strode over to GR. "That Totter, he was supposed to take Yvonne out tonight and he stood her up."

Yvonne blinked and rubbed under her eyes with the back of her hand "It's alright, really it is," she sniffed and quickly looked to make sure that no one was watching her, which of course they were.

"Don't worry luv. We will get you a lift home, you'll see." GR took the two empty teacups from Eileen, "I'll go and get you a cuppa." He joined the throng of customers around the coffee stall. "Hey Lew. Want a prettier passenger?"

Lew looked at the girl, liked what he saw, and at the same time felt sorry for the youngster. "Ok, but what about Jesus?" he nodded towards the longhaired figure cracking jokes with the law.

"Don't worry. Gurn can give him a lift."

Lew left to introduce himself to his newly acquired girlfriend.

Jesus left his new friends and went back to the lads by the stall. He combed his unfashionable long hair and pulled the loose strands from his steel comb. "Well, what are we going to do about a kaff then?"

"The Joyburger down Garrett Lane has just opened. That might be ok." Gra carefully combed his Tony Curtis styled hair. The hair cream showed white on the teeth of the cheap plastic comb.

GR pocketed his change and watched as the man at the coffee stall poured out a stewed cup of tea. "Too near home, and I don't fancy being too near the Henry Prince Estate mob neither."

"Don't worry GR. Think of our reputation. If need be I'll take them on by myself and leave you chappies to play tiddley winks." Cecil's head disappeared into his jacket as he attempted to light a fag. "Hey Gra. I've run out of lights, have you got a match?"

"You're face and my --" Gra stopped, it wasn't worth it. He'd only lose again. He chucked a box of red heads over. Cecil took a dozen or so out and returned the box.

"I know a place near where I work at Putney. We could try there." The static in Jesus' hair made it stick to the comb, the street lights glinted in it making a rainbow.

"Well I for one fancy a slow ride." Cecil struck a red head on the zip of Gra's jacket, and, with much huffing and puffing, got his roll up alight.

"All stick together," said Gurn pulling on his helmet and buckling it up. "Make it look good."

Graham commenced to pump his reluctant Arrow into life.

"Impress the natives eh?" Foxy tried to buckle up a borrowed helmet that was far too big for him, managed it after a fashion, and headed for Gra's bike. "And no dragging, remember: We are young motorcyclists, not Rockers."

Jesus pulled on his silk inner gloves and then his fur lined gauntlets. He mounted up behind Gurn on the old, but well kept, Triumph T100. "Coming GR?"

GR shook his head "Got better things to do." He collected Yvonne's cup of tea and set off to rejoin Lew and the girls.

The three bikes lined up together.

"Don't forget; no dragging. I'm the only one that knows where this place is," Jesus shouted to the others. They nodded in acknowledgement.

The three bikes dragged off.

There were two scooters outside when the lads pulled up at their destination. Gra looked dubiously at the row of neat terraced houses. "Jesus, are you sure this is a kaff?"

"They call it a coffee house, but it's the same difference really."

The lads boxed in the scooters and followed Jesus into a small house. The interior was plush, there were carpets on the floor, there were low seats with large cushions scattered on them, central heating, and soft music, and there were even fancy light shades. All except Jesus stood there stunned.

"This is a kaff?" hissed Gra.

"If yer don't like it, yer don't 'ave ter stay." Jesus had already taken his helmet off and was attacking his jacket with its accompanying layers of jumpers.

"Nah, nah." Gra joined the strip show. "Get us a cuppa Cecil, and don't bother with any pies. My teeth still hurt from the last one."

"And one for us, chorused the others.

"Five teas luv."

"No teas, only coffee." A tall dignified woman, accompanied by her doe eyed daughter stood behind a bamboo covered counter.

"Oh well, give us five coffees then, and not too gentle on the sugar." Cecil was a bit put out about the tea, but after a shrug settled himself to finding a dog-end in his cavernous pockets. He pulled out a battered, oil covered specimen, and lit it with a red head he had struck on the counter. Doe Eyes eye's grew even larger. Cecil winked and gave her a leery smirk "'ello darlin'. Where you bin all my life?"

She fled into the depths of the kitchen. Mother returned with the coffee "Ten shillings please."

"Ten shillings? Ten shillings? I asked for coffee, not caviar!"

She fixed him with a stern eye, "Ten shillings."

Cecil picked out the money in the smallest change he could, and carried the precious liquid over to the table where the others were seated. The others found his experience a huge joke, and made no effort to hide it.

"Wots up, Issac my son?" Foxy stroked his nose, "Oi vey, did you have to spend some of your shekels then?"

"It ain't bleeding funny. Ten bob for five bleeding coffees. She's the Shylock, not me. I mean, I only earn three pound ten a week as an apprentice."

Jesus pouted his lips and made smoochy noises, "Ahh, did didums have to put his itsy bitsy fingers into his pursey worsy and take out some of his likul pennies then?"

"Ahhhh," chorused the others in mock sympathy.

Cecil poked two fingers at them and sat down to enjoy his expensive drink.

"Flash, eh!" Graham leaned his chair back on its two back legs, causing much creaking. He looked around for an ashtray to engrave, but found they only had crystal glass ones. Not to be disappointed he turned his attention to the radiator on the wall.

The Mods in the corner opposite were watching the lads intensely. Graham took out his adjustable spanner and tried the security bolts on the radiator: the three Mods' jaws fell. Cecil was watching, the effect had not been lost on him, and he too took out an adjustable spanner. The other lads joined in the spirit of the game. The end result was that the table was soon covered in a collection of what the Police often called 'Deadly Weapons', but which the lads regarded as essential tools for the oft unreliable motorcycles they rode. The Mods blanched, and went into a huddle. Graham found it a big joke and started making ferocious faces at the intimidated Mods, the other lads soon got bored. Cecil took off his boots and lay back on a luxurious couch, covered himself with cushions, and went to sleep.

Foxy went off to find the jukebox. He looked everywhere, he even tried to trace back the wires from the speakers, but drew a blank. He approached the Mods cowering in the corner, "Where's the jukebox then?"

"Eerrh, jukebox, err, well, er there ain't one."

"There ain't a jukebox? Where's this insipid music coming

59

from then?"

"Well it's, er, it's piped. Yes, it's piped."

"Can't we change the music then? That's a bit much, ain't it?" Foxy walked back to the lads muttering to himself. The daughter was dusting a table. As he passed Foxy gave her a friendly pinch.

"Aaaaahhhhh. Mummmm meeee."

"Cheeky, ain't she," said Graham, gently easing the sleeping Cecil's many pairs of socks off of his feet, and hiding them under the table.

Jesus had decided that the table would look better with 'Honda' engraved on it. Foxy had taken over Gra's job of intimidating the Mods.

Cecil woke with a scream as Graham lengthened the flame of the cigarette lighter he was holding under Cecil's bare foot.

The woman reached for the phone.

"I wouldn't do that if I was you."

She looked up, expecting to see vicious leather clad beast threatening her with a spanner. Instead she saw Gurn's mild face, his blond hair tousled like a schoolboy's.

"We'll be going now, and I don't think we'll be back. It's not really our style, this place." His soft Cornish accent reassured her, and she replaced the receiver. "Come on lads. Let's go."

"Where to?" Cecil's voice was muffled as he groped under the table in search of his missing socks.

"Back up the Bridge to collect L.T.2, then to the Joyburger, I suppose. Or maybe just home."

"Come on then," Gra started to tog up. "And Cecil, stop flashing your arse. You are making those boys," he indicated the Mods, "those boy's mouths water."

"Good night luv."

The lads trouped out.

"Good night darlin', give us a kiss," Graham lunged after the daughter. The others dragged him out backwards.

Chapter 7: DAY TRIPPER

"Morning lads," Gurn pushed out the side stand and lent the Triumph Tiger 100 over.

GR strolled over and prodded the precariously balanced pile of bags tied to the pillion seat of Gurn's bike. "Looks like you need a camel more than a motor bike."

"Does a bit, still never mind I'll put it in Lew's sidecar or the L.T.2."

They wandered over to where the other lads were leaning against Lew's front fence. Both of them gave a wide berth to Mick's bike as it swayed gently in the breeze, the bent centre stand making a crunching sound as it rocked from leg to leg.

Graham's dad staggered out of his front door, "Eh er ah oh ah."

"Hastings for the weekend, dad," confided Graham, being very careful to keep down wind of the cider fumes.

"Ach ner mm eh argh."

"And enjoy yourself too dad."

Mr. King made several attempts to mount his rust encrusted push bike, and eventually succeeded. Despite the riders many attempts to fall off, the bicycle wove its ragged path down the road, up the pavement, and down the road again.

"Mum, dad's off," yelled Graham.

"Then pick him up," wailed back a thin voice.

"Now Vernon; have you got your tent?"

"Yes Ma."

"And your sleeping bag?" Lew looked at the mottled, water stained roll at his feet. "Well?"

"Yes Ma."

"And your spare jumper? And your clean pants, and socks?"

"Yes Ma."

GR sauntered up "Hey Lew, don't forget your hot water

bottle, and your teddy bear, and, of course, your dummy."

Lew shoved past him none too gently.

"Where are you lads going then?" enquired Lew's mum.

"Hastings."

"Oh, I would have thought you'd be going to Brighton. It's so much nicer at Brighton."

Foxy looked up from the brake shoes he was playing with. "Ah, well, Brighton ain't our lucky place. Last time we went there we parked the vehicles and marched down the street. Coming up the other way were about 300 Mods. So, rather than waste time working out the odds, we turned round rather sharpish, marched back to the machines, and got out as quickly as we could with out losing too much face. Bit of a waste really. At least we can expect a welcome at Hastings. All the lads go to Hastings."

Lew's mum looked at Foxy dubiously. Foxy went back to getting L.T.2's brakes fixed. Even if L.T.2 wouldn't start, at least it would stop, or slow down, or drift to a halt, eventually.

Gra and Gurn started to load up L.T.2 and the sidecar Lew had recently fitted to the Velo.

"Oi get that junk out of my chair."

Gra looked up from trying to shove an over filled kit bag down the nose of the sidecar.

"Wots up? Frightened the floor will fall out?"

"Viv's got to get in there."

"Put her on a diet. Anyway, she's Totter's hot water bottle, not yours. Let him take 'er."

"Not everybody can get the day off, just to get away early."

"Can I 'elp it if I was taken sick?"

"If yer want ter start yer convalescence at the seaside you'd better give us a hand ter get these brakes fixed!" yelled Foxy, his white teeth making a marked contrast with his blackened face.

Viv wandered up from the bus stop, dropped her bag on the

already large heap, and stood around looking pretty. "'ere, are you two going in for a job with the black and white minstrels?" she ducked the shower of stones that Foxy and Gra aimed at her, and joined Gra's girlfriend, Sue, on the back seat of the car.

"Are we ready then?" Foxy wiped his face and hands with a dirty rag, making them blacker than before.

Gurn pulled the elastostraps on his rear carrier up and pushed his over-mittens between them and his bag, "We've been ready for the last hour."

The lads finished stowing the bulk of the luggage into L.T.2, and the remaining baggage, including Viv, into Lew's sidecar.

BANG, crackle, POP.

"Sounds like someone has been feeding his bike rice crispies!" GR looked up as a familiar bike pulled in. Gurn winced as he recognised his once cherished and immaculate Tiger Cub in a now somewhat reduced state. A skinny youth in a leather jacket two sizes too big for him and a pre Boer War crash helmet that could only serve to keep his ears warm, sat astride the steaming mount, the sun creating rainbows in the dripping oil. Thick smoke wafted in the once clean air as the oil found the exhaust pipe.

Lew looked over in the direction of the apparition. "Oh, by the way, this is Methanol Pete. We work at the same place."

The youth nodded to the lads, who in turn nodded back and made a note that Methanol Pete could not have squeezed another blackhead onto his face, no matter how hard he tried; there just wasn't any room left.

The bikes were prodded into life, and Foxy herded his passengers aboard the L.T.2.

"All wave to Mrs. Barrett," shouted Graham.

"Who's Mrs. Barrett?" Methanol Pete asked, in all innocence.

A front room curtain moved the house opposite side of the green in front of Lew and Gra's houses.

63

"Oh, of course, THE Mrs. Barrett."

All the lads waved, and the face behind the curtain disappeared.

The convoy pulled into the muddy field. It had been a funny day, warm sunshine, rain, and now sunshine again.

"There's a nice place, near enough to the other lads for mutual protection, but just far enough for us to have some privacy." Foxy drove over to the camping area, leaving the others to park the bikes in the car park.

GR pulled his overloaded bike onto its centre stand, and walked over to Lew's sidecar. "Oi, Sambo."

Lew looked over malignantly; the Velo losing its front mudguard had not improved his temper. The mud the front wheel had thrown over him had not improved his face.

"Oi, Sambo. Want a hand to unload then?"

"Yeah."

GR withdrew his arm up his sleeve, took off his glove, and looked for the missing member. "That's funny," he continued to search both the glove and up the sleeve, "it was here a minute ago."

"I'll tell Cecil you've been pinching his jokes."

"Even better," rejoined GR, "tell his Great Grandfather. That's where he got them from."

They fell to unloading the chair, leaving the others to unload L.T.2, and to put up the few patched, and dilapidated tents that they had managed to scrounge.

GR woke up for the umpteenth time, but this time the red glow of his eyelids told him that day had broken. "Oi, Mick."

"Grunt, grunt."

"I can't feel me feet. In fact I can't feel anything from the knee down."

"As long as it is only from the knee down, you're all right."

Mick tried to wriggle his toes, but they wouldn't move. He tried to bend his knees, but they wouldn't move either. He found that the whole of his legs were numb. "If we have contracted a strange virus that has crippled us, do you think they'd give us wheelchairs with Bonnie engines on the National Elf, GR?"

"Why?"

"I can't move my legs either."

GR cautiously opened an eye, and peered at his feet. They weren't there. "Oi, Mick. I think someone has pinched me feet."

Mick slowly opened his eyes, looked under his lashes, and then opened his eyes fully "Snow! Snow at Easter? Snow?"

The wind whistled through the torn fly of the tent, causing flurries of snow to dance round the lad's knees. GR Pulled himself out of his sleeping bag, and put on his leather jacket and crash helmet to make himself fully dressed. He fumbled with numb fingers, and found the Gaz stove, lit it at the tenth attempt, and warmed his hands. "Cup of hot chocolate?"

Mick nodded, and started to dress himself by putting on his leather jacket and crash helmet.

GR scooped up two cups of snow, put them on to boil, and searched for the tin of pre sweetened instant chocolate. "With, or without?" he held up a tin of sweetened condensed milk.

"Oh, with please." Mick carried on clearing out the snowdrift.

GR spooned out two generous helpings of condensed milk into each cup. Mick's helping was with the ants, grass, and dirt; his own without. Carefully he mixed the brew, and then joined Mick up the dry end of the tent. Slowly the warmth permeating the chipped tin mugs thawed out their hands.

Mick nodded towards a motorbike fitted with a double adult sidecar that was framed in the open fly of their tent.

GR studied it. "Spinx, a fellow ex-inmate of Stalag Sex at

65

Southfields. Actually I'm surprised to see it here. Usually he talks about his bike, but rarely does it ever materialise."

The door of the chair opened, and out got the sparse figure of Spinx.

"Wots the matter Spinx? Cold or something?"

Spinx poked up two fingers, and headed for the toilet block. The chair door opened again, and out got Chris, "Mornin'."

"Mornin'."

Then out got Nutta, "Mornin'."

"Mornin'."

Then Megga, "Mornin'."

"Mornin'."

"That's the way to keep warm," said Mick, "body warmth."

"I'd rather keep warm the same way as Gra and Totter," GR nodded towards two of the tents that poked out of the snow.

"You'd better keep clear of Totter this morning GR."

"Why? I helped him to put his tent up when he got here late last night." GR blew hot air down the front of his jacket. "It wasn't easy in the dark either."

"Yeh, but you knew where the guy ropes and the tent pegs were when we let it down on him and Viv in the early hours of this morning."

"Well, why should he have all the fun? The dirty lecherous, lucky, bugger."

Lew and Methanol Pete emerged from their tent and sneaked up on L.T.2. On the count of three they threw open the doors to reveal various bodies in assorted yoga positions. Everyone stirred as the freezing air hit them, everyone that is, except Foxy. Lew made a snowball and jammed it on the steering wheel in such a position that, when it melted, the drips would go up Foxy's nose.

Slowly the camp came to life, and slowly the lads headed for the men's toilet block, girls and all.

In the bog Totter turned on the hot water taps, and like

everyone else took to warming himself on the hot water pipes. Those still waiting their turn sat on the toilet pans and stamped their feet, and chaffed their hands together. Totter turned his head, "Wot's the time?"

Lew looked at his battered heirloom "Six."

"Right, as soon as Foxy wakes we're off into town." Totter stuffed his now warm hands into Viv's pockets as they were warmer than his own.

"So soon?" GR didn't want to leave his nice warm cubicle until he had to.

"Look dummy; the man who collects the camping fees comes round at seven, so everyone goes into town by half past six."

A yell of rage and surprise echoed round the camping ground.

"Ah. Sounds like Foxy's awake. Right let's get going." Totter led the others out towards the tents so that they could prepare for the departure.

"Here, Lew. Got this just for you." GR passed over a peaked cap with an L.C.C. badge on it.

"Where did you 'arf inch this from? A School Keeper?"

"No. I ain't a tea leaf. He gave it to me."

Lew folded the top of the cap in half and bent the peak down so that it looked like a S.S. reject. GR put on his own peaked cap. A work of art this; complete with desert goggles, and more badges and chains than even his leather jacket possessed. The two strutted over to the bikes. The two motorcycles on either side of Mick's lay on the ground. GR lifted his bike up, Mick's bike waved to him, and did a little victory dance on its warped centre stand.

A blue-nosed, and tired looking Gra leaned out of L.T.2 as it chugged past "Wee oh, wee oh, ... yawn ... . All down to Danny boys ... yawn."

"Too much bed and not enough sleep," grumbled a jealous Mick as he joined the queue of bikes that were slowly filing out the gate and onto the slush covered road.

The convoy followed a tortuous course down the winding narrow country lanes, and then onto the narrow winding streets of the old town of Hastings, until they reached a tiny fisherman's cafe on the seafront. Foxy led the way in, past the crowded tables and chairs. He tilted his head back to see under the peak of his peaked cap, "Har, hah, me hearty!"

The man at the counter gave Foxy a look of disdain and flicked his fag ash over the row of clean cups in front of him.

"Give us a cup of tea lad, har hah, and shiver me timbers." Foxy stood on one leg and closed an eye in what he felt was a reasonable impersonation of Long John Thomas.

"You sure you don't want a cracker for your parrot an all?" the man behind the counter drawled in his soft Sussex voice.

"He's crackers enough as it is mate," chimed in a blue nosed Lew.

The lads queued up and collected a cup of tea and a slice of burnt toast each. Graham ordered a big fried breakfast for both him and Sue.

Sue tucked into the mass of fried eggs, bacon, fried bread, and chips that lay on the big plate in front of her.

Foxy sat opposite. "Urh, urh," he pointed a finger into his mouth, "urh, urh."

Sue threw a chip into the gaping orifice. Foxy collapsed in a fit of coughing, his face going an even brighter shade of red than that of the tomato sauce with which Graham had drowned his meal. In fact Gra was having difficulty in eating his reddened food as he had a head on each of his shoulders, and one on his lap. The heads panted, and hung out their tongues. Gra smiled, and made each mouthful last longer than the previous one.

The door opened and two fishermen came in. They stared at the lads, and appeared to be amused at their appearance. The lads stared back, they too were amused, particularly with the gold earrings the fishermen sported. "Well, what 'ave we got

68

'ere then? Some of them there Rockie Rollers from Lundun? "

The lads returned the complement by shouting out; "Take yer 'ands off me crutch Jim lad.", "Har, hah, get the last apple out the barrel Tom," and other known nautical sayings.

"Polly wants a cracker, Polly wants a cracker." Foxy ducked as a rock hard crust flew at his head.

"What time does the Club house open?" Gra enquired of no one in particular.

Spinx, seeing Gra's attention diverted, seized his opportunity, and dipped his toast into Gra's egg yolk.

"Eight. Anyone here members of the aforesaid Club?" Foxy counted three. "How many of us?" he counted again, "Twenty."

"That's alright, three cards should be enough."

Fred Funnel, the proud proprietor of the camping grounds, stood in the doorway of the Clubhouse. The tassel on his fez bobbed constantly as he tried to see who, and how many were trying to get in. "Are you boys all members then?"

"Members and guests Fred, members and guests." Foxy looked up at the rotund figure and waved his membership card.

"There's only one guest per member. You ain't bringing that lot in here on one ticket."

"Oh no Fred." Foxy looked deeply shocked. "This is my guest," he indicated to Mick. Fred nodded and they went in; the ticket went back down the line.

"Here you are Fred," Spinx and Totter went in, each with a guest, meanwhile the tickets went back to the waiting lads stamping their frozen feet in the entrance.

GR made to enter with a guest.

"'Ere, I've just seen that ticket," protested Fred.

"Yeh, well, he's me brother," GR indicated Totter, who had already settled down in the corner of the hall. "So the name's the same, ain't it."

Fred looked at Totter, then at GR. The height was almost the same, the hair was almost the same fair colouring, the build was the same, they looked somewhat similar, but, but Fred Funnel wasn't sure. Whilst Fred pondered GR and his guest walked in and the ticket made its return journey down the line. Fred was sure he was being fooled somehow. "Right, you Rockie Rollers; you yobodie hois. You get into pairs then, and you keeps apart." He had them now. "I don't want none of your Lundun tricks 'ere."

The lads did as they were told. Three tickets were produced and six entered. The others stood near the entrance, wondering how they were going to get in.

Foxy came over, "What's up Fred?"

"'e ain't a member, 'e ain't got a ticket."

Foxy had his back to Fred and kept strong eye contact as he slipped both his card plus one other on to Pete.

Pete tipped back his newly acquired cowboy hat with 'Kiss Me Quick' on it, and smiled at Fred in a patronising manner. "I didn't say I wasn't a member Fred, only that I hadn't got a ticket." He fiddled in his back pocket. "But I've found it now." Pete held up Foxy's card. Fred squinted at it, trying to make out the name hidden beneath the dirty finger marks on the card.

"'ere," Fred turned to Foxy. Pete and his guest sidled past slipping the card into the back pocket of Foxy's jeans, the other card had been passed back down the line long ago. "'ere you. That were your ticket, that were!" Fred smiled triumphantly

"No it weren't Fred," Foxy produced his card with a great flourish. "You know, I'm worried about you Fred. I think you need new glasses."

Two lads slipped behind Fred's back, he turned to yell at them, but they had vanished into the throng of leather clad lads that filled the lower end of the hall. He turned back to interrogate Foxy, but he too had gone. The last two lads went past him into the hall "Hoi, where's your ticket then?" One of them held up a card, his thumb placed over the name. Fred waved them on, he felt he had been cheated. He wasn't sure how they had done it; but then he knew them Lundun boys were cunning, not like the locals. He had the local's measure all right.

The lads settled in the corner by the jukebox, turned the radiators on full, and settled down to the serious business of getting warm.

"Wots for dinner GR?" enquired Mick.

"Irish stew, peas, baked beans, and spaghetti. Just stick it all in a saucepan, and heat it up. No trouble. We'll live like kings while the peasants," GR tilted his head back and peered through his sun glasses at the other lads, "while the peasants starve."

Mick wandered off to examine the billiard table at the other end of the hall to see if it could serve as a substitute for table football.

"Oi, Mick. What are you doing for grub?" Lew examined the coin mechanism on the table.

"Oh, we've brought a lot of tinned stuff."

"Lucky you, not having to live on toast and the smell of an oil rag, like the rest of us." Lew found the mechanism tamper proof and gave up. "I'll give you a word of advice though; friend to friend. Don't let GR do the cooking. Went camping with him once, he even managed to burn a tin of baked beans. I hate to tell you what he did to the rest of the grub."

Mick thanked Lew and went over to the counter to buy some Milk of Magnesia tablets.

Footsteps echoed down the hall, the lads round the jukebox looked up as a man in his late twenties came towards them.

"Hey, Foxy." GR squinted under the peak of his cap, "That bloke coming towards us was talking to Fred earlier and pointing to us. Do you think it's trouble?"

Foxy took his feet off the radiator and turned to look "Nah

71

that's Fred's son-in-law. Almost one of the lads he is." Foxy took off his peaked cap so that the son-in-law could recognise him better.

"Mornin' lads. Cold in't it," the son-in-law's teeth chattered the same tune as the lads' teeth.

Gra proffered an oil stained packet of baccy "Like a fag?"

Sue felt Graham's head to check that he was feeling ok.

"Ta. No music then?" the son-in-law gesticulated towards the jukebox with one hand as he expertly rolled a fag with the other. "Don't tell me you Lundun folk is broke? I thought the streets up there was paved with gold?"

"That's the horse shit." GR took Gra's baccy from the son-in-law and rolled a cigarette the thickness of a matchstick.

"Oi, a fag, not a bloody cigar!" Gra tried to snatch the packet back, but GR had already passed it onto Lew.

"Tell you what," the son-in-law sat down on the table, being careful to sit between the puddles of cold tea, "tell you what, I think we will have some music on, something nice and noisy. Fred don't like noisy music." He produced a bunch of keys suited to the Tower of London, got off the table, and opened up the front of the jukebox. Gurn looked at Foxy, but Foxy just shrugged and continued to roll a fag from Gra's baccy. "There are," the son-in-law beamed, "anything you like, so long as it's noisy. Cos Fred ...."

"Don't like noisy music," interrupted Spinx as he took the baccy from Foxy.

"That's right. You've got the idea." The son-in-law walked off jingling. "See you later then."

"Give it a try" Gra told Pete, who was nearest the buttons on the jukebox.

"Don't mind if I do." Pete took the baccy from Spinx with one hand, and pushed a load of buttons with the other.

"From a Jack to a King," sang the jukebox.

"What did you push that one for?"

"I didn't. Still never mind, it's free."

"Is it?" asked Gra as he peered into his empty baccy packet.

Gurn surveyed the fast melting snow from the window. "Makes the place seem a bit livelier."

Foxy tipped back his head to see under the peak of his cap. "You wait till the locals get here, it really livens up then."

GR was playing with the penny ball machine on the wall by the bogs when a sudden commotion by the entrance made him look up. A dozen leather clad youths were arguing with Fred, and by the passing of cards behind backs were obviously up to the same trick as the lads had employed that morning. One of the youths sauntered over to where GR was standing.

"You must be one of them Lundun lads then?" He nodded towards the penny machine causing the dewdrop to fall off the end of his blue nose. "Enjoying yerself then?"

GR took off his sunglasses so that he could see his questioner better in the evening gloom "Not bad. It's only cost me a tanner for an hours entertainment."

"That's expensive," said the local. He removed his hands from his pocket and lifted the machine off the wall. "'ere you are" he rummaged inside and gave GR back his money. "There's no point in wasting money, is there?" The local put the machine back on the wall and slowly walked over to the tables that the other lads were occupying, leaving a bewildered GR still staring at the ball machine. The other locals had by now finished bamboozling Fred and joined the swollen ranks of lads.

"How's the music situation then?" a hulking six footer asked Foxy.

Foxy, who was standing, looked the seated giant in the eye and gave him a wink, "The son-in-law had a look at the jukebox for us."

"Won't last. Fred don't trust him any more than he trusts us."

73

The son-in-law came over with the bunch of keys at his waste jingling. "Fred's gone all suspicious, says I've got to look at the music machine," he gave the jukebox a friendly boot. "Been watchin' you he 'as, for six hours. He reckons he ain't seen you lot put a penny in whilst the machine 'as sung its 'ead off. If weren't for the fact that you've kept on playing 'From a Jack to a King', he'd 'ave said somethin' sooner. He likes that tune, does Fred." The son-in-law plunged his hands into the internals of the jukebox and rummaged about making the thing crackle and bang. "He says you're cunnin', you Lundun folk. Not like the locals, he's got their measure," both he and the locals gave a cackle. "Oh well, must be off. Don't forget now. Don't go kicking it or anything," he booted the front shut, and headed for the bar.

"Oh well," the giant got up and patted Foxy on the head, "better put on some music." He put a shilling piece in, stood back, took careful aim, and kicked the jukebox in the left-hand corner, about a foot off the ground. Quickly he pushed as many buttons as he could, being careful to avoid Fred's favourite. "Should keep things going for an hour or so."

The jukebox gave a crackle; "From a Jack to a King ....."

Slowly the hall filled up. The lads, local and visiting, occupied the lower half of the hall by the stage whilst everyone else was crammed into the other half. The lads sitting listening to the beat music, had just finished doing an obscene version of the hand jive called 'The O'Sullivan', when a jingling sound told them of the return of the son-in-law.

"When you lot going to 'Buffalo' then? Fred don't like you lot 'Buffaloing'. Reckons it's dangerous."

"What about them?" GR indicated the ordinary campers up the other end of the hall.

"Well" replied the son-in-law, "you lot is the cabaret as it were, sort of free entertainment."

"Better sort ourselves out then."

Spinx put a bob in the jukebox, kicked it in the appropriate place, and pressed the buttons for all the fast tunes. Whilst the music machine played, 'From a Jack to a King' the lads split into four teams, one local, three visiting.

"Oh well," said the son-in-law with a smirk, "better go and tell Fred not to worry as you ain't goin' to do it tonight."

Some of the unselected lads cleared the dance hall, and the teams lined up in Indian file, two teams to each end of the hall. Sounds Incorporated started to play 'William Tell', and the teams limbered up. Each member faced sideways, crossed his ankles, bowed his knees, bent his elbows out, and marked time, the elbows going up and down in rhythm with the heavily booted feet. The floor shook, and glasses rattled at the concerted efforts of the four teams, each ten strong.

POUND, POUND, POUND. "Buffeeloooooooooooo," yelled Foxy at the rear of the first team, and it thundered off with Lew at its head.

"Buffeeloooooooooooo," screamed the Captain of the rival team at the other end of the dance floor.

"Wee oh, wee oh."

CRUNCH

The two teams collided, elbows on, sending bodies flying everywhere. Spectators rushed in to pull the wounded off the floor.

"Buffeeloooooooooooo."

"Buffeeloooooooooooo."

The other two teams headed for each other at a fast pace, elbows going up and down at a frantic rate. They missed. One team ended up in a heap as they piled into the tables and chairs at the campers' end, spilling enough beer to float a battleship. The other team collided with the stage.

"Buffeeloooooooooooo."

The first team set off again, this time with Gra at its head. The leader of the local team craftily changed direction, and hit the visitors at an angle, bowling the rear-half of the column over. Gra and the other front runners rammed through a side door and into the ladies' bog.

Water came to Fred's eyes, although whether it was the sight of two more teams lining up to Buffalo, or the thick fog of cigarette smoke in the hall, only he knew.

It took half an hour for the last of the able bodied to become crippled. Gratefully the survivors slumped into their seats to revive themselves with liquid refreshments.

"Oi, Shylock. I'm going to get a beer, are you coming?" asked Jesus.

Lew looked up from massaging a bruised knee, "Nah, just changing hands." He delved into his crowded pockets, found a creased and grubby pound note, and joined Gra and some of the others at the bar.

"'ere."

GR looked up to see one of the locals standing in front of him "What?"

"'ere, come outside with me a minute."

GR eyed the lad suspiciously from under his peak.

"It's alright," assured the lad, "I just wants an 'and like."

GR got up, adjusted his cap, and followed. As they got to the door the local lad picked up a coke bottle from a table. "Better bring one of these."

"Why?" GR was still suspicious. In London lad didn't fight lad, but in the provinces? He wasn't so sure. They might be like the Teds of old, always fighting each other.

"It's alright, really it is. I don't want no fight or nothing. "

GR picked up a bottle and followed him outside, not knowing what to expect.

Two Mods were on the step pestering a girl. The local lad grabbed one, stuffed him up against the wall, and waved the bottle under his nose. "Leave 'er alone Kokenut, or you'll lose yer virginity to this 'ere bottle."

The Mod blanched "Who says I want to rummage with summat you've rummaged with. I don't want to catch nothin'."

"That's my sister!" The lad gave the Mod a prod in the solo plexus with the bottle. The other Mod went as if to help his mate. GR stepped in the way and tapped the empty bottle into the palm of his left hand a couple of times. The Mod looked at him; GR stood with his back to the light, the dim illumination served only to give a dull reflection of light off his multi-badged leathers and peaked cap. He looked very sinister, like something out of a cheap American crime magazine. The Mod changed his mind.

"So, you leave, 'er alone." The lad assisted the first Mod into the fresh snow with the tip of his boot. The second Mod gave off looking at the menacing image of GR, and scrambled away to help his reaching comrade.

"Thanks for the hand," said the lad, none the worst for his bit of exercise. A white faced GR nodded, shivered, and went back into the hall. He headed straight for the bar. A stiff drink was what he needed.

The crunching sound of the lad's boots in the snow as they approached the bog woke Mick up. He got up off his pan, stepped out of his sleeping bag, and flushed the cistern to wake up GR who was dossed down in the next cubicle. GR struggled out and joined Mick around the steaming hot water in the hand basin. "We got time for a cuppa before we go into town?"

"Sorry my son, you'll just have to spend some shekels and buy it." Mick moved out of the way as the other lads and the girls piled in and turned more hot water on. "You see, my little sleepy head, it's half past six already, and it's time we were off."

Gurn turned the cold water on for a drink, but nothing happened, the pipes were frozen.

Foxy drove up in L.T.2. "All aboard. Come on, come on, all

what's going. Load up while I go and splash me boots."

A dozen or so piled in while the others went to the bike park and started to wipe the snow off the saddles.

"Where are we going to?" GR asked in a cloud of vapour. "Danny Boy's?"

"To start with, until it gets crowded, then it's off to that flash place on the prom for another cuppa or three." Foxy tightened the silk scarf round his neck and, with much twanging of springs, settled himself on the driver's seat.

GR slipped the chain of his peaked cap over his red and purple blotched frozen chin. "Alright for those with money."

"You'll find something to do GR. You'll amuse yerself, some 'ow." Foxy planted his foot, L.T.2's wheels span, and it lurched off, sending up rooster tails of snow.

GR sat in the side road watching the traffic. There were scooters everywhere. He'd already carved up more of them in the last half-hour than he usually did in a whole week. The rumour that the Mods were heading to Brighton for another riot was, as usual, wrong. The Mods were obviously on a tour of the south coast. GR determined that they weren't going to have it all their own way.

Four scooters went past in a flash of colour and chrome plate. The riders, in their ex U.S. Army parkas, were leaning back as if their backs were broken. GR pressed the starter button, and the Honda Super Hawk screamed after them.

The bike shot alongside the scooters in a matter of seconds, and GR laid it across the nose of the lead scooter. He braked to 30 m.p.h. and dropped the bike down into second gear, the needle of the taco hovered just below the red line. They tried to overtake, he saw them in his mirrors and pulled across in front of them. They tried the inside, he flicked the bike the other way. Down to twenty, and into first. Two of the scooters tried the outside again. GR let them come almost alongside, then screamed the bike across their noses, taking them over to the other side of the road. He poured on the power till he saw a side road and pulled into it and waited for the four scooters to pass by. They pottered past, the riders looking nervously about. GR gunned the Honda again and screamed past them to dive in and slam on the brakes. The scooters pulled into the curb, the Mods turned off their engines and dismounted. A disappointed GR did a quick U turn, and did a couple of slow passes in an attempt to get them to come out and play, but they weren't having any of it.

The door of the restaurant opened "Taxi!" GR pulled in, and Foxy mounted the pillion "To the bog, James."

They roared off.

The square in which the public bog was situated was packed with row upon row of scooters, hundreds of them. GR pulled up at the bog, and both he and Foxy got off. Mods were everywhere, like ants. "Into the Valley of Death rode the five hundred." Foxy stood at the top of the steps and surveyed the subterranean Mod bog.

"You've forgotten something Foxy, there ain't five hundred of us, only two."

"All the more glory." Foxy adjusted his peaked busman's hat, stuck his hands into his pockets, and sauntered down the steps with GR in his train. The Mods made way, the lads made water, then left as unhurriedly as they had entered.

"Thank God for the reputation," said a relieved GR as they climbed the stairs out into the sunshine.

"Which must be preserved at all costs," Foxy reminded GR as they mounted up. "Better make it a quick trip GR, there are others who want a leak." Foxy gave a couple of Mods the Nazi salute and almost fell off as the bike ripped round the square.

GR sat in a side road watching the traffic. 'Six bog runs,' he pondered 'and not one hitch, the Mods must be getting soft'. A dozen of them came out of a shop and mounted their scooters.

GR started the bike and pulled out into the main road. They saw him, turned off their engines, and went back into the shop. There wouldn't be any more fun this morning, perhaps they would have forgotten him by tomorrow. He rode up to the fountain at the end of the prom. Two of the local lads overtook him as he poodled along. The bikes in front slowed down. As they rode round the fountain the girl pillion riders threw something into the water, then the bikes roared off again. GR tried to puzzle out what was going on, and had just given up when the first detergent bubbles started to appear. The locals were in a playful mood, so there was bound to be fun when they came to the club that night.

As GR pulled away the fountain started to take on the appearance of an iced wedding cake.

The clubhouse shook as the big tipper truck pulled into the car park. A tall skinny lad got out of the cab and dropped the tailgate. A dozen lads buffaloed into space and landed, with varying success, into the soft mud.

"Don't use your bikes much then?" Methanol Pete asked one of them as he extricated himself from a muddy puddle.

"Can't drink and drive."

"What about the driver?" Pete stuffed his gloved hands between his knees to stop them knocking.

"He can't drive anyway, so make no odds really."

As they all sauntered in Fred put on his fez and went out to check their membership cards. He saw who it was, thought better of it, and sat down again, muttering.

A lot of people were at the club tonight, couples were jiving and twisting to the beat music, their only respite coming when the jukebox played an unselected 'From a Jack to a King'.

Foxy came over to the long table most of the lads were seated round. He looked pleased with himself. "Hey GR, do us a favour." GR looked up, wondering how he was going to get out

80

of this fight. "I've got this bird lined up, but she's got a mate." Foxy shrugged his shoulders, "Well this mate rather fancies you, funnily enough."

"It ain't funny. She's just got good taste, that's all."

"Anyway, as I was saying, she's got this mate with a warped sense of humour, and I was wondering if you would do me a favour, and help out."

"That type of favour I'll do anyone." GR removed the damp newspaper he had stuffed into his boots, and started to pull them on.

"What about Eileen GR?" asked Gra.

"Her and Big G are supposed to be going to Brands on Easter Monday, so two can play at that game."

"Did she tell you this then?"

GR stiffened, clicked his heels, and put on his best German accent. "Nein, but ve haf vays off finding zees things hout. Mind you," he slipped back into English, "whether she goes or not is another thing. Very unpredictable is Eileen."

"Don't tell me, I know. Her sister was the same." Gra moved closer "Mind you when she was in the right mood, she'd get up to some funny things. One night I got her up on Ham Common and she ...."

"What are you talking about luv?" Sue tweaked Gra's thumb back against the joint.

"Ahh, ergh, ehh, me bike darlin'. Now please let go of me bleedin' thumb. Argh." Gra doubled over into Sue's lap.

GR left them to it. He didn't like violence. He made his way over to where Foxy was waiting.

"This is my girl," Foxy put his arm around a cute looking fifteen year old, "and this is yours."

GR looked at the girl he had been introduced to. "We have met." He held out his hand, and the four of them left the hall. "Tell me," GR whispered in the girl's ear, "is your brother always so protective towards you?"

"Only where Mods are concerned. He worries about the family honour."

GR smiled. The jukebox finished playing 'From a Jack to a King', and started to play 'Ticket to Ride'.

Fred got onto the stage, and banged the top of the table with a beer bottle "Tonight is Saturday night." The Beatles sang on, drowning his voice. "I said," Fred shouted, "I said, tonight is Saturday night."

"and I don't care" called back the Beatles.

"Turn that bloody thing off." Fred crossed over to where he could yell at the lads. "You Rockie Rollers, you've had that on all night. Turn it off!"

The son-in-law came over and thumped the jukebox in the side and it lapsed into silence.

Fred looked up and gave a rare smile, realised what he had done, and replaced it with his usual scowl. "Tonight is Saturday night, and Saturday night is ....." The silence was deafening. "and Saturday night is....." Still silence. "Why Bingo night." Fred's annoyance showed in his voice.

"Bongo? What's Bongo Fred?" enquired a lad.

"You means Bingo. Why Bingo, that's where I calls out numbers, and youse marks them off on a ......" Someone sniggered. "You, you yobodie hois, you Rockie Rollers, you're havin' me on. That's what you're doin', why don't you get to the other side of town, where you belongs?"

"Go on Fred, don't be a spoil sport. Let's play this Bingo of yours."

"Yeh, go on. Give us some excitement."

"Well," Fred started to count heads, and also the potential profit, "well, alright then. But you'd better behave yourselves. I've got the measure of you lot, I 'ave."

Amidst much pushing, shoving, and carrying on, the lads moved tables and chairs into rows facing the stage. Fred stuck the Bingo cards into his back pocket, and went down to collect the money.

"How much Fred?" Graham sifted through the collection of loose change in his hand.

"One shilling."

"Not bad Fred. A shilling for a nights entertainment."

"A shilling a game, young man." Fred adjusted his fez, and gazed with disdain at the Cowboy hats Gra and Sue were wearing.

Sue looked up at Gra with a twinkle in her eye, "I'll give you a game for a shilling."

"You mean a night's entertainment for nothing," Gra snorted.

"Nothings free." She took a coin from Gra's paw and passed it to Fred.

Fred took two cards out of his pocket, and gave them to Sue. Totter took two cards out of Fred's back pocket and gave one to Viv. Fred collected the dues, handed them to the son-in-law, and remounted the stage. "If you'd all like to sit down."

The lads sat down, anywhere and everywhere, including on Fred's seat and table. "Down there; in them seats." Fred gesticulated wildly causing the tassel on his fez to bob frantically. "I don't want no nonsense from you lot." He glared at the lads who replied by poking up two fingers, and with other friendly gestures. "You yobodie hois, I've got your measure."

The lads sat at the front. The campers sat behind, where they had a better view of the lads and could watch the entertainment.

"Right." Fred turned to the son-in-law, who had been counting the proceeds and removing the bank's not insubstantial percentage, most of it into his own pocket. "How much in the kitty then?"

The son-in-law ground his fag out in a pool of spilt beer, and surveyed the collection in front of him. "Two pounds, three shilling and six pence. Plus three francs, two polo mints, one metal washer, and a Japanese coin of indeterminate value."

At the mention of the last item Gra searched his pockets, and found his lucky coin missing. Sue smiled to herself; it would give him the will to win.

"Eyes down, look in for a full house."

"We ain't West Indians Fred. We don't 'ave full 'ouses," Spinx insisted. Several of the lads stood up and gave Nazi salutes. Fred banged the beer bottle on the table to restore order, the bottle exploded. Tears welled in Gra's eyes as the golden stream flowed over the stage and dripped onto the dance floor.

"Order, order." Fred pointed the neck of the broken beer bottle at the fanatical Spinx who still stood at the salute. "You. You there. You get to the other side of town, where you belong."

"Oi Fred," a voice cried out. "Fred your flies undone."

Fred bent down to look, Spinx seized his chance and changed places with a lad a couple of rows back. "All right, all right, you Rockie Rollers, let's get on with the game." Despite a visual assurance that the information on his fly was incorrect Fred still gave the zipper a reassuring tug with his free hand whilst menacing the lads with the bottle neck in his other.

"I thought this was the game?" Viv said to Totter.

"Actually it's illegal," replied Totter as he started to unscrew the leg of the table in front. "Fred baiting was banned at the same time as bear baiting. But old habits die hard." He stuffed the screw into his already crammed pocket.

"All the fours," announced Fred.

"Drop your drawers," chorused the lads.

Fred went to say something to the son-in-law, but he didn't appear to have heard anything unusual, so Fred changed his mind. "Two and nine; why that's the ....."

"Brighton Line."

"Do you Rockie Rollers want to run this game, or do you

84

want me to run it?"

A slow handclap started.

"Get on with it" Gra called out and several campers nodded in agreement.

"Clickerty click....."

"O'Sullivan's dick," called Totter, who was well up on his Bingo calls.

Fred ignored him. "Two and six, that's half a crown."

"If I give you half a crown, will you get your knickers down?' sang the lads. "If I give you three and six, will you let me suck your ....."

"ENOUGH!" Fred went to bang the table with another beer bottle, but decided not to risk it. "ENOUGH! I will get the Police in, I will."

"What, and have to admit you ain't got a properly kept visitor's book?" Methanol Pete reminded him.

The lads eased off, and the next dozen calls went without a challenge. Fred gained confidence.

"Four and three."

"Stre - aw – berry." A lad near the front got up and took a bow, acknowledging his nickname. Half a dozen beer bottle tops flew around his ears.

"Seven and two."

"Up your flue."

"Flat."

Fred looked up. "WHAT?"

"Bungalow."

"Eh?"

"Maisonette. I mean house" Gra climbed on to the stage accompanied by a couple of others. Totter, complete with screwdriver, moved into Gra's place at the other end of the long table.

"You ain't got all these 'ere numbers." Fred looked Graham in the eyes, the bobble on his fez balanced on the end of his

85

nose like an obese fly. Spinx moved a counter on Fred's master copy.

"Yes I have Fred," insisted an indignant Gra.

Fred looked down. "That's funny. But you ain't got number eighty one though, have you."

"Nor have you."

Fred looked down at the master copy and then commenced shouting, "You yobodie hois, you've been cheating."

"How could we Fred." Gra put his hands on Fred's shoulders and looked down into his eyes "You've got our measure Fred, haven't you." Pete picked up the full bottle of beer on Fred's table, and passed it to Lew who put it inside his leather jacket. "You just need new glasses, that's all Fred." Gra scooped up the winnings, put one of the polo mints into his mouth and the other into Fred's "How about another game then. I'm enjoying this."

It was two hours before Foxy and GR snuck back into the hall. The two girls went into the Ladies to tidy up. The lads were also tidying up after the marathon Bingo session.

Foxy put his silk scarf back around his neck to cover up the love bites. "Any luck at the Bingo lads?"

"As much as you had, by the looks of it." Lew, who most people trusted, counted the takings. Gra, who nobody trusted, watched and rubbed his hands. "Between us and the other lads, we only missed one game. This," Lew prodded Gra in the guts, causing him to fall backwards off his chair, "this twit got the giggles and moved the wrong counter. Still I suppose it was only fair to let the campers win one game. After all it was mostly their money."

Pete came over with a tray of drinks bought with the proceeds of the first game. "Just goes to show what you can do with teamwork, as they used to say at school." He watched GR who had taken off his cap and was massaging his jaw. "Enjoy yourself GR?"

GR stopped what he was doing, and took to fingering a swollen lip "Tell me Pete. Have you ever tried to have a passionate snog with an electric food mixer?"

The two lads lifted up the last long table in front of the stage. The legs fell off. Fred shook his head in dismay.

"Ah Mr. Funnel." Totter strolled over, "I have just the thing for you." He delved into his pocket. "A set of near new, long reach screws, only been used once, and that by a man with little interest in sex."

Cecil, Big Ray, Moonie, and the other stay at homes entered the club wearing their newly acquired cowboy hats. Fred showed no interest in them, he was beginning to wonder if he really did have the measure of the lads.

Foxy watched their entrance from under the peak of his cap "It took you lot long enough to get down here. Anyone would think you had come from London."

"Alright Scoffer Fenwick," Big Ray went over to the stage and started to scrape the mud off the inside of his boots on the stage steps. "The town is crawling with Mods and cops, took us ages to get through."

The girls sat near the radiators and lit up, leaving the lads to go and get the teas.

Jesus came in with a plump girl in tow.

"'ello cheeky" said Gra as he assessed the girl from behind. Sue pushed his hat over his eyes.

"Oh, yeh," said Jesus "This is Isabel."

"Necessary on a bike?" some wit called out. The bored look on Isabel's face showed just how many times she had heard that joke.

"Glad to see that you've volunteered," exclaimed Cecil as he led a protesting Jesus out the front door. "Stree-aw-berry, who knows this area like the back of his girl's fanny, is taking us walkies."

Isabel gave a half smile, and joined the other females by the window.

The chill air outside contrasted sharply with the tepid warmth of the hall. The camping grounds looked like a deserted First World War battlefield. The fast melting snow had turned the whole field into a sea of mud, and the whole sodden area was covered in deep puddles. The volunteer trekkers gathered in the car park.

"Where's the Tokyo war horse?" GR looked around for Jesus' little Honda Benley Sports.

"Sold it to pay a speeding fine. Got a real fast machine to replace it though," Jesus indicated a battered old outfit fitted with a coffin box for a sidecar. "My uncle gave it to me. He used to use it to transport his racing bike to meetings."

"A racer eh?" said GR sarcastically. "Suppose it's got all the gears, close ratio box and all that?"

"Wide ratio, actually," they joined the others who had gathered round a smiling Stree-aw-berry. "You see second gear doesn't work."

"Never mind, at least it's got a nice colour scheme. I always did fancy a bike in olive drab and racing rust."

The girls were looking out of the window, white gulls circled and swooped over the bleak landscape, a few pockets of snow glistened in the glen. A loud clamour at the club entrance announced the return of the adventurers. All were soaked and covered in clinging brown mud. All except Stree-aw-berry, who had led the trek on account of the fact that he knew the area like the back of his girl's fanny. Some of the lads thought that perhaps he was still a virgin, the more cynical thought that perhaps he had been too familiar with girlfriend's anatomy for their own good.

The lads hung up their steaming jackets, and stuffed old newspaper into their boots to help dry them out. Someone took a scrap of paper out of his jeans pocket and passed it to Spinx. The dirty poem amused him, he read it and passed it on, adding a scrap of paper of his own. Soon everyone was reading various pieces of paper that contained everything from pornography to political lampoons.

"I once had a copy of Eskimo Nell," confided Foxy as he finished reading 'A thousand and one ways of doing it'. " Someone pinched it though. They are as rare as hen's teeth. Not many people know that poem, only snatches of it."

"I know the whole thing off by heart," said Spinx. "Thought the telling of it makes me thirsty."

Foxy took the hint and put some coins on the table. Others followed suit, and Pete went off for the liquid supplies. When he returned Spinx tested the golden fluid to check on its suitability. Being satisfied he began:
"When men grow old,
    And their balls go cold,
    And the end of their knob goes blue.
    When it's bent in the middle,
    Like an unstrung fiddle,
    They can tell you a tale or two.
    So buy me a drink."
(Guzzle, guzzle, guzzle)
"Find me a chair,
    And a wondrous tale I will tell.
    Of Dead Eyed Dick, Mexico Pete,
    And a whore called Eskimo Nell."
(guzzle, guzzle, guzzle)
"Now when Dead Eyed Dick, and Mexico Pete,
    Went out on the range for fun:
    It was Dead Eyed Dick who used his prick,
    And Mexico Pete the gun."
(Guzzle, guzzle, guzzle)
Spinx slurped his way through the epic tale, and finally

slurred his way to the end. The lads applauded, both Spinx's memory and his beer capacity were far beyond that of ordinary mortals. Spinx smiled, bowed, and passed out. They laid him in state on the table, his leather jacket under his head, his hands crossed, and a filched plastic flower covered in dust on his chest.

GR surveyed the rows of empty glasses at Spinx's feet. "That's quite something," said Mick, who had been chatting up a couple of birds and had missed the whole telling, "and that one," he pointed to a nice looking girl with assisted blond hair, "fancies you. I'm going out with the other one, so you can do us a favour by making it a foursome."

"A favour like that I don't mind doing." GR smiled as he strolled over to his new girlfriend. He knew Mick's little game, but Eileen was out of Mick's reach, at least until he managed to buy a brand new bike."

The floor was packed with people dancing. Those lads with a girl did the creep, those without did 'The Lad'. Everyone was enjoying themselves, even the campers found enough room for a quick jig.

Fred came over and turned the jukebox off at the mains. Nothing happened. The son-in-law thumped the side and the sound from the jukebox lost volume slowly until there was silence.

"Oi, what's going on?" Lew asked.

Fred climbed onto the stage where three balding, middle-aged men wearing light blue satin jackets were setting up music stands inscribed 'The Texans'. Fred cleared his throat for an important announcement. "Urghmmm. Tonight is Sunday night, and ....."

Pandemonium broke out "Where's ada musica?" called out a local lad.

"Oi, Mustapha Crap, put the jukebox back on!" Gra insisted,

egged on by the others.

Fred pulled out a referee's whistle, carefully picked out some fluff from the mouthpiece and then blew on it as hard as he could. The effort made his eyes stand out like two giant pickled onions. The shrill sound gave way to silence. "Tonight is Sunday night, and Sunday is?" Silence. "Is?" Even deeper silence. "Is music night!" said an exasperated Fred.

"We already had music. Turn the jukebox back on," Gra insisted extracting himself from Sue's embrace and making for the stage.

"Yeh, put the box back on Fred," Methanol Pete added, putting his half empty beer glass down.

"Tonight," Fred continued, "is music night, and to provide the music, by popular request ...."

"Of a rival establishment?" queried Stree-aw-berry.

Fred ignored the interruption, ".....by popular request, are the Texans. A big hand for the Texans!" His request was met by the deepest silence of the night.

The pianist came over to the microphone at the front of the stage. He tapped it, the microphone wobbled precariously. He blew into it, the telescopic stand contracted as if offended by his beerey breath. He pulled the reluctant stand back up, "Testing: one, two, three."

"What comes after three?" asked Lew, wondering if the dim looking pianist really knew the answer.

The pianist went to reply, but stopped. He had played here before. "Now for the first dance, we are going to play a quick-step." He resumed his seat.

"One, two ...." the guitar started. Drong, drong.

"Three..." the drummer joined in. Bum, titty, bum, titty.

"Four..." the pianist started playing. Plink plonk, plink plonk.

"He's playing like the bloke with one eye!" protested Lew, but the other lads didn't hear him, they were too busy watching Foxy, Totter, and Cecil do a fair mime of the band.

91

"And now," said the pianist, "we will do a rock and roll number, for our friends down here." He smiled at the lads, the lads sneered back.

Drong, drong: bum, titty, bum, titty: plink plonk, plink plonk.

"Do is the operative word!" stated Lew as he disgustedly headed to the bar for a replacement drink, feeling that alcohol might deaden the pain of listening to the music.

Mick listened hard to the tune and then made the profound statement: "It's the same tune."

"It's the only one they know," Foxy informed him. "Ain't it mate."

The pianist recognised Foxy from an earlier visit and quickly looked the other way.

On the dance floor the young couples crept round, locked in an embrace and insensible to the music, their thoughts on better things.

"And now a waltz," announced the pianist.

Drong, drong: bum titty, bum titty: plink plonk, plink plonk.

The lads got up and started to do their version of the conga.

"De dah dah dah dah daah, Oh!"

"Form a circle," cried Cecil from the front of the line. "Form a circle."

They headed for the bar. Fred headed them off. They headed back towards the stage, recruiting lads and campers as they went. The Texans stopped in mid plonk.

"Well seeing as you don't like that one we'll play a quick step," said the pianist as he shuffled his bum on the threadbare piano seat.

Drong, drong: bum titty, bum titty: plink plonk, plink plonk.

The lads and the campers formed a circle and started to do the Hokey Cokey.

"Oh, Hokey Cokey Cokey."

"Wee oh, wee oh."

The circle contracted as the two sides rushed at each other.

They stopped just short, then drew back.

"Oh, Hokey Cokey. Wee oh, wee oh."

The circle again contracted. This time the two sides met, bodies flew everywhere.

"Err, now another waltz?" asked the now rattled Texan pianoman.

"Knees up Muvver Brahn
Knees up Muvver Brahn
Under ver table you must go
Ee yi, ee yi, ee yi, yoo.
If I catch yer bendin'
I'll 'ave yer knickers orf ...."

Fred blew his whistle "Do you lot of yobodehois," the campers involved in the riotous cavorting gave Fred a black look. "Err, beg pardon. Do you, err, people want music, or don't you?"

"Yeh," Spinx went over to the jukebox and thumped it on the opposite side to that thumped by the son-in-law earlier in the piece. 'From a Jack to a King,' it sang out.

Couples started to dance again. The Texans went to the bar to drown their sorrows.

"Can I sell you a copy of the War Cry?" A Salvation Army officer stood by the table and peered through the cigarette smoke and beer fumes at the lads.

"Jesus Christ," exclaimed Gra as he looked up.

"No; only his representative." The Sally Ann man smiled.

Lew removed the man's peaked cap and replaced it with Gra's cowboy hat. The man laughed, sat down with the lads, and chatted with them. When he went to leave the lads delved into their now almost depleted pockets, and put some money into his collecting box.

"I don't know what the Rabbi will say when I tell him what you have done, Isaac my son," Cecil helped himself to the money in Foxy's hand and put it into the box.

Fred came over to make sure that there was no trouble brewing. "I hope these Rockie Rollers ain't giving you no trouble. I keeps telling 'em to get to the other side of town where theys belongs."

The Sally Anne man tipped back the cowboy hat, saw who it was, and stuck the box under Fred's nose. Fred put in a two-franc piece.

"And on that happy note, we will love you, and leave you." Cecil and company started to tog up for the return to London.

"Not tonight you won't, I've got piles." Gra chimed. Sue gave Gra a withering look that only served to make him collapse in hysterics.

"See yer scum," Cecil called out cheerfully from the doorway.

"Day tripper, yeah," screamed the jukebox.

"And 'From a Jack to a King' to you too mate." Jesus put his arm around Isabel and followed the others out.

GR and Mick were saying good-bye to their respective girlfriends. GR looked odd as he was not wearing his peaked cap, but rather his crash helmet, the first time he had worn it in four days, except to sleep in that is. The other lads were breaking up camp and loading up the junk. They had spent the morning dodging the fee collector, and it was now a cold snowy 2pm.

"Are we keeping together on the way back, same as we did on the way down, or are we all going our own way?" Methanol Pete pulled a darned woollen scarf over his frozen nose.

"Better keep together in case of breakdowns." Lew looked up from the improvised hearth comprising of three bricks in a broken oblong where Foxy was putting out the blowtorch that had heated the water for the final cuppa.

"Thought it was a bit cold for those on bikes to hang around meself." Chris exercised his knees; sleeping four up in a sidecar was taking its toll. Those that had finished their chores came and warmed themselves by the improvised stove.

"Come on you lot, get 'em down. Let's be off." Gra tipped the dregs of tea from his mug onto the bruised grass.

"You ain't talking to Sue now you know," Foxy reminded Gra.

Slowly everyone got ready to move.

"You've got my address?" the bleach blond girl asked.

GR nodded, "Sure."

"You will write?"

"Sure."

They kissed, clung together for a moment, then parted. GR went over to his bike, cleared the snow off of his saddle, sat down and pulled on his over-trousers. Mick did the same, his bike fell over sideways as the centre stand finally broke.

"God pays debts without money," GR said as he surveyed the broken end of his front brake lever.

"Tally ho."

"Wee oh, wee oh."

The convoy pulled slowly out of the car park and down the road. They were about five miles out of Hastings when the solo motorcycles broke away from the group - it was far too cold for them to hang around. By the time they were ten miles out, the treacherous conditions caused the pace to slacken. Only Chris and GR continued to speed. Chris followed in GR's slipstream. Eighty, eighty five, slow and lay it over for a sweeping curve; feel the back end go; bring her up; get traction; lay her over again being careful not to give her too much throttle too quickly; feel the back end break away again; pull her up; lay her over again. Straighten up to come out of the bend, wind her on past a couple of cars, watch the slosh, lower your helmet to take the slosh on the peak, clutch hand off to wipe your goggles. Chris watched GR, he was not taking the best lines through the bends and could have gone faster on the straights.

Chris twisted back the throttle and took his Triumph T 110 to the ton. As he went past GR waved him on. Chris held his nose up as he went by, to add insult to injury.

Fifty miles gone, Chris was cold and his fingers were dead and had been for ages now. His hands were dead too, that was bad. Clutchless changes up were all right, but changes down were another thing. His feet were dead also, that too was bad as it took a super effort to change gears or operate the rear brake. His face was ok, the facemask saw to that, but his eyes were burning from the freezing draft that came in his goggles. The fact that his knees had set and he would have difficulty in getting off his bike, let alone walk, didn't worry him unduly, but the draft down his neck did. He fidgeted to reposition his woollen scarf, but failed. He slid back on the saddle and adopted a more streamlined crouch over the tank. His layers of jumpers rode up and let the cold in at his back. It was no good, he'd have to stop somewhere. 'Godstone' said the sign post. Chris could see a cafe with a few bikes outside it. He decided to pull in.

The bike coasted to a halt on the gravel surface of the car park. Two lads who were outside the café helped Chris off his bike and inside. Chris sat down at the table and held the cup of tea in his two hands. Slowly, painfully, his circulation returned, setting his whole body throbbing. Outside GR droned past on his way home.

It took the best part of an hour before Chris felt like making a move. He had just reached his bike when the convoy pulled in. Spinx was in Lew's sidecar. There were at least two extra passengers in L.T.2, and one of the solos was showing signs of crash damage.

Foxy came over to Chris swinging his arms as he came. His breath hung about him in a cloud. "Nice time we had at Fred's eh! Have to go there next holiday."

Chris watched as Lew and Pete made running repairs with

frozen fingers to Lew's outfit "Aye, provided we can muster the transport."

Chapter 8: SHOT OF RYTHM AND BLUES

It was a warm night and the air had a smell of summer about it. GR and Eileen were walking home from the Joyburger. Eileen was in a bubbly mood, GR however was in deep thought. He wasn't happy about the Joyburger, it wasn't a bike 'kaff'. There were Mods there and of course the Henry Prince Estate Mob. Already that lot had brought in the Police with their fighting and thieving. Still it was handy having a base within walking distance of home when you'd dropped your bike and it was off the road. GR looked sideways at Eileen, who was trying to blow smoke rings and laughing at her own efforts, and wondered how much longer he would have her company with his machine off the road for at least a week, maybe two. Perhaps it wouldn't have been so bad if she hadn't been on the back when it had happened. Oh well, having a girl who went fifty/fifty with the petrol wasn't everything. The sound of a bike caught their attention and they both looked round to watch.

"Totter and Viv." GR studied the line Totter took for the S-bend. "It's the right line, but he's going far too fast; he'll never make it".

Totter came up to the first road island and really cranked it over round the tight right hander sending up a stream of sparks from the silencer of the venerable Bantam. Going far too fast, he took the bend wide and didn't leave himself enough space for the left hander. He twitched the bike hard over. The back wheel slid away, the centre stand dug into the tarmac and the bike jerked upright. Viv stepped off. The right side of the bike hit the second road-island causing it to jump. The bike did a full somersault and landed on its opposite side, skidding across the other side of the road, dragging Totter with it.

GR and Eileen ran across to Viv who was sitting in the middle of the road none the worse for wear. "Why didn't he get off?" GR yelled. Viv shrugged and joined the other two as they rushed to where Totter was lying beside his bike.

"Evening GR," Totter looked up and surveyed the scene. "Have I done anything to the bike?" The two girls pulled Totter onto the pavement.

GR uprighted the battered bike and pushed it down an alley. He came over to Totter and gave a noncommittal grunt. "So so. How are you?" Totter looked down at his right knee where blood was welling through his torn jeans. The sodium lighting made the blood look a dirty brown and almost unreal.

"Oh." Totter tried to get up. His head swam as shock started to set in. He tried to get up again and almost passed out. He waited for the world to stop going round. The blood oozed thickly from his leg and onto the paving stones. Totter looked up and smiled wanly. "Looks like the old stitches have burst again. I always did do things in style."

GR turned to Eileen who was looking the other way and still trying to blow smoke rings "Oi, Puff the magic dragon." She looked over, being careful to keep her eyes off of Totter's leg. "Get back to Joyburger, fast. Get Lew to bring the sidecar and tell him to leave the back off. Totter will have to keep his legs straight." Eileen ran off, glad to be gone. GR and Viv tried to do what they could to stop the blood.

It was a long five minutes before the bikes arrived. Carefully Lew and Foxy helped Totter to hobble across to the sidecar. Lew had removed the back and Totter sat in it facing backwards with Viv behind him to give him support. The lads inspected the damage whilst the loading operation went on and removed the broken glass from the road.

"Shouldn't we have a red cross on the chair or summat?" asked Gurn.

"At least it won't cost me fourteen bob for an ambulance," Totter called across to Lew who was performing acrobatics on the kick start.

"That's what you think Isaac." The old bike coughed into life, Lew put it into first gear and pulled off, his motorcycle outriders forming up around him.

"Surely Lew won't charge him?" asked an incredulous Eileen.

"No, the hospital will though, ambulance or no ambulance. I once had a crash on an emergency run I was doing for a hospital's blood bank. Delivering urgent blood samples. I walked to the hospital, despite the injuries, to hand over the samples. They still charged me, the Shylocks." GR pulled Totter's bike up from the wall it was propped up against. "Oh well, better take this home and put it in the front garden."

Eileen lit another fag and inhaled deeply. "Yes, let's go. I've had enough of crashes to last me."

Cecil looked down and surveyed his new suede brothel creeper boots. Even if he hadn't got the bike fixed, at least he could go down to the Joyburger and show off his new Ted's shoes to Foxy and make him go green with envy. He waited at the Earlsfield lights for a break in the traffic and had just decided it was a lovely night for walking when someone shouted, causing him to look round.

"Hey, mate, you going to the Joyburger?" Cecil saw a young lad not more than sixteen, astride an ancient but well cared for Triumph sprung hub.

"Perhaps, why?"

"Want a lift?"

Cecil hadn't got his helmet but thought 'What could happen in a quarter of a mile?' He walked over to the youngster, "Thank you my man." He sat on the pillion and found a handhold under the saddle.

The lights changed and the youngster carefully pulled off. The old bike had cost him his last penny to buy and he had to look after it. Two old ladies looked at the lads as they rode passed. Cecil put on his haughty look and gave them the Royal wave.

The prospect of the Henry Prince S-bends on a sprung hub Triumph, the original whip iron, was daunting, but the youngster took it very carefully. They were just sweeping out of the second bend when an old Morris van pulled out of a side road and blocked the way. Instantly both lads knew they wouldn't stop in time. The youngster changed his line in a vain attempt to go round the van but, with a crash that could be heard for miles, the two vehicles collided.

Time slowed as in a dream. The rider looked on as the van did a double somersault beneath him. How high he seemed to be. He watched as the block of flats slowly span into and out of his vision. How slowly things happened, he wondered how he was going to land, and he wondered what the damage to his bike would be. Time resumed its normal pace as he heavily hit the pavement.

The bike had stopped sliding and Cecil, who had got a foot caught, had been dragged along the road with the machine. He wasn't feeling too happy. "My poor shoes. Four bloody quid and now this." He extracted his left foot from under the bike and noticed the shoe was cut off clean across the toes. He looked again; his big toe was hanging by a few threads of skin. "My toe, my toe!" He called across to the young rider: "Help me, I've cut me bloody toe off."

The youngster was too busy looking at the white shinbone that poked through a ragged hole in his jeans.

"Go on, ask them." Mrs. Glover gave her husband a shove, "Ask them."

Her husband looked down at his feet "I don't know how they

100

will react. Brian's my son, I know how to handle things with him, but these others, they are a load of roughs. I don't know about them."

Mrs. Glover gave her husband another shove "Go on. They are nice lads really."

Mr. Glover approached the lads sprawled outside Lew's place. Most were cleaning the bright work on their bikes, a few inspected the repairs GR had made to his Honda. "Err, hello boys."

"Afternoon Mr. Glover," Totter sat on the kerb defying anyone to trip over his stiff leg. "Anything we can do for you?"

"Err, well, err I wondered if you boys would go and visit my son in hospital?"

Gra stopped polishing his bike and stuffed his handkerchief back into his pocket "We'd be glad to. We wanted to go before but thought we'd best leave it to the family. We didn't know if we'd be welcome."

"Err, yes, well after a week of nobody but us, he's got more than just a bit bored."

"Don't worry," Gra put a dirty hand on Mr. Glover's new beige raincoat, "We'll cheer him up for you."

The silence of the ward was shattered as the lads pulled into the car park outside, two of the duty nurses stood at the window giggling and pointing.

CRUNCH, CRUNCH. Two dozen boots echoed through the building. The ward sister looked up from her desk and saw the invaders advancing on the door of the ward.

"Only two to a bed," she called out. "Only two."

Little Ray shrugged, "Never did fancy playing three in a bed anyway."

"With a face like yours you're lucky if you can get anyone to go to bed with you," Foxy snorted.

The lads marched on.

101

"The sister said only two to a bed." A petite Chinese nurse tried to stop the flow, she succeeded only in stopping Foxy who was about her own height. The others poured passed.

Foxy looked around, "That's all right. There are lots here who ain't got any visitors. We are just making up for them. Anyway, how about you and me making it two to a bed?" Eileen grabbed Foxy's collar and pulled him after her.

Cecil turned to face the lads. He looked a cross between Dracula and Frankenstein's monster. The dried blood and plastic skin on his face was peeling off in places and lifting in leprous patches in others. His eyes were narrow slits in yellow and purple fields and his two front teeth were missing.

"Evening Ces, you're looking well." Foxy inspected Cecil's bandaged foot. Eileen looked away and lit a cigarette.

"Can we smoke?" asked Lew.

Cecil muttered, the scabs on his face made speaking very difficult. It sounded like a lot of gibberish.

"Good, where's the baccy then?" Lew rummaged in the bedside locker.

Jesus took off his helmet and put it over Cecil's bad foot. "Grapes. That's what people need when they are in hospital. Anyone think to buy you any?"

"YES THEY DID." Cecil indicated an over-flowing fruit bowl.

"Oh ta." Jesus took a large bunch and sat at the end of the bed to eat them, spitting the pips decorously into the waste bin at the other end of the bed.

"Oranges too, how thoughtful. All that Vitamin C does you good it does." Totter took two and sat down stiff legged on the bench seat to peel them. Gra, who wasn't so greedy, only took apples for himself and Sue.

"At least he's got good company, ain't he GR." Big G tapped GR on the shoulder and pointed to the group around the youngster who had given Cecil the lift, but GR and Yvonne were too busy to notice the interruption. "I said he's got good company!" Big G shook GR's shoulder.

GR broke away from Yvonne to see what the commotion was all about. The youngster was lying back listening to a pirate station on a transistor radio while a couple of his mates played naughts and crosses on his plaster cast. Another couple played with the winding mechanism of the bed. "Times have changed since the Boys Brigade, but I see you're still in uniform," GR addressed a huge leather jacketed gorilla who was busy polishing his boots with the curtain.

"Evening. Yes still in uniform. I hope you are behaving yourself. The minister doesn't like it if any of his little flock go astray."

"Oh yes, I've been a good boy."

"That's a matter of opinion." Yvonne clung possessively to GR's arm. GR looked across at his ex-Boy's Brigade associate, winked and returned to his unfinished business.

"I don't like orange drink," remarked Jesus, his head inside the locker. "Ain't you got anything else?"

"Pass it here. I ain't particular," Foxy had already acquired a glass.

"We've got some lemon and barley," volunteered the gorilla.

"Good. Nice to see someone with taste." Jesus manoeuvred round Pete and Gurn who had taken on the youngster's mates at naughts and crosses on the lad's plastered leg.

Cecil went to take some fruit out of his bowl and found it was empty.

"Do you want a pear, Rocker?" A Mod across the ward held up a large fruit. "Here ya are then." He tossed the pear high in the air. Cecil caught it. The over-ripe fruit collapsed in his hand, the juice trickling down his arm.

"They are getting over bold ain't they?" Lew rolled another fag from Cecil's baccy.

"DON'T BE GREEDY WITH MY BLOODY BACCY."

Lew looked at Cecil, "Quite right." He passed the baccy over to Foxy.

The Chinese nurse gave a yelp and glared at Gra whilst she rubbed her backside. Sue also glared at Gra. Cecil looked innocently at the ceiling and silently whistled a pretty tune.

Foxy glared into the fruit bowl, "All gone! You greedy little boy Cecil." He let go of Eileen's hand. "I'm going to visit some of those poor old souls who ain't got no-one to talk to." He wandered off to a sad looking old man opposite, "Hello Grand-dad. Want someone to talk to?"

"Hello son. Want some fruit?" the old man indicated a bowl with some over-ripe specky apples.

"Oh ta. Want a fag?"

"Time please," cried the Ward Sister.

Lew looked at his battered heirloom with the cracked lens, "Half past seven."

"Time you bought a watch?" suggested Jesus.

The lads started to move off. GR went up to Cecil and, after rolling a fag, gave Cecil back his baccy. "Be a bit awkward changing gear on your Eyeti spaghetti burner." GR poked the bandaged foot. Cecil winced.

"I'VE FINISHED WITH BIKES"

"Oh yeh? Oh we'll see you around then. By the way, you might get a visitor later on." GR put his arm round Yvonne and followed the others out.

Gra went over the Mod who had generously given the overripe pear to Cecil. He surveyed the tackle attached to the Mod's plaster cast "I bet that's uncomfortable." Gra gave the plaster a rap with his knuckles, "Needs adjusting too." He hoisted the leg up until Mod was flat on his back. "See yer."

The ward had just returned to normal when a motorcycle pulled in. The Ward Sister slammed her pen down on the desk, "Right, I've had enough," she stormed out into the passage. A leather-clad figure with a white crash helmet was surveying the ward through the glass window of the door. "All right my lad, I've had enough nonsense for one day. Don't think you're going in there. It's well after visiting time."

The figure turned. Grey hair poked out from around the helmet and softened the rigid features of the man's face, the light reflected off his well starched dog collar. "I'm Bill Shergold. I believe two members of my youth club are in your ward." He gave a gentle disarming smile.

The sister went red and averted her eyes "Oh yes, well err reverend, err father, err vicar, if you'd like to come this way."

Chapter 9: IF YOU'VE GOT TO MAKE A FOOL OF SOMEBODY

The two nuns stood in the gateway to the school, the hot sun burnt through their black habits making them feel very uncomfortable. The younger of the two was talking in a very thick Irish accent. "Tell me Sister, have you not seen the new roster? Why I think it's terrible. Sister Theresa was saying to me only this mornin' .... " She looked intently at her companion who was looking across the road and did not seem to be listening to her. "Sister, were you not hearing what I was saying? Sister?" she followed the others gaze.

Down the side street opposite a tall slim youth wearing sunglasses sat astride a gleaming motorcycle. Except for his helmet and scarf he was clad entirely in black leather. The few movements he made caused the sun to dance on the badges and intricate patterns of studs that covered his jacket. The gentle breeze played with the bright orange scarf that hung over his shoulder; sometimes it jumped, only to fall back into place; sometimes it flicked shyly over his arm. Light arrowed off the highly polished bright work of the bike causing the whole image to shimmer in the hot air giving the scene an air of unreality. He watched them.

A bell trilled loudly and green uniformed girls poured out of the school buildings laughing and shouting, causing the birds to fly into the trees for refuge. One of the girls broke away from the flock, and with little regard for the traffic, ran across the road to where the youth sat. His face betrayed no emotion as she put her overflowing briefcase onto the saddle and climbed on the bike to sit a-top the case. With no visible movement on the part of the youth the bike coughed and burbled into life. He lifted his hand in mock salute to the nuns, pulled in the clutch and snicked the bike into first gear. The taco hit the red line before he dropped the clutch and the bike screamed into the main road, the front wheel pawing the air like a frightened pony.

"It's terrible, terrible," said the Irish nun. "A nice girl of ours, going out with one of them. Did yer not see the colour of his scarf? Orange it was, orange."

Her companion watched as the bike disappeared in the traffic, the rider's scarf fluttering in the slipstream "Yes it is terrible, very terrible." But she was thinking not of the boy, or the bike, but of her own lost youth.

"Slow down GR, slow down," Yvonne shouted over the noise of the bike.

GR turned round to see her trying to keep her balance on the twisting bike, one hand on her Panama hat, the other trying to keep her skirt down. He smiled humorously. "If I'm going to get you home, changed, back to my place, fed, and onto the speedway in time to meet the other lads, I've got to get a move on." He did, however, slow down.

"And tuck your scarf in. It's all over my face," Yvonne yelled. He did so. "And why you bought an orange one I don't know. Why not a nice white one like the rest of the lads wear?" He turned and smiled without humour, she giggled. "Never mind GR, I still luv's yer."

They wove through the traffic on the Embankment, passed the moored houseboats, and through into Fulham and the back streets. They came into the grounds of the flats, and slowly wove through the parked cars till they reached Yvonne's block. She got off, upsetting the briefcase and its paper contents. She bent to pick them up while GR put his bike on its stand.

"You'd better come in while I change."

"Oh good. I like strip shows." GR rubbed his hands together.

Yvonne opened the front door and entered "You should be so lucky. You can sit in the front room with mum and dad."

"Whoopppeeee."

Mum and Aunty looked up as GR entered, and suddenly found something to do in the kitchen. Dad looked up unsure of himself. Mum came back in with a cup of tea in an old china mug. GR sat down in an armchair and drank it.

"Eerr, umph, you and my little girl going steady then?" dad's eyes blinked rapidly.

"Oh yeh. I suppose you could say that," GR crossed his legs, the highly polished .303 rifle cartridge on the suspended boot waved to and fro throwing light beams around the room.

"Err, well, err. I hope you are being good." Dad glanced at GR who gave a puzzled frown. "Err, you know, not playing around that is. Err, umph, we don't want any little troubles." Dad blinked a few more times. "You know? Course you know what I mean. Don't you?"

"Oh, that. Oh yeh I know what you mean."

Yvonne appeared at the door adjusting her helmet, "Ready GR?"

GR nodded to Yvonne, then turned to dad: "You don't have to worry Mr. Berry. I won't get up to nothin' I shouldn't. I give you my word as a good Catholic on that."

The troubled look left Mr. Berry's face, he smiled. GR put on his orange scarf and winked. Mr. Berry looked troubled again.

"Ain't you two got nothin' better to do?" Foxy put his hands in his pockets and jingled the loose coins.

GR and Yvonne disentangled themselves from each other's arms. "Oh hello Foxy. Where's the car?" GR brushed his fair hair from his eyes.

"Funny you should ask that. It has passed on to richer pastures."

Yvonne straightened her clothes, "Where's Eileen?"

"Funny you should ask that. She's gone on to richer pastures too."

GR looked down at Yvonne, who had slipped her arm around his waist "Hard luck isn't it."

"Yeh. Oh well," Foxy pulled out a grubby packet of chewing gum which he offered to the two lovers, "a girl who goes 50/50 with the petrol money isn't everything. By the way; the funeral for L.T.2 is at Plough Road Baths, midnight on Friday."

A small line of bikes appeared and Foxy quickly put the packet of gum back into his pocket. "Evening."

The lads dismounted and took great care to ensure that their bikes were securely locked up. Methanol Pete in particular was securing his scruffy old outfit in no uncertain manner, the chain he was using looked as if it had originally come off an anchor.

"By the way Pete," Mick called over from where he was trying to jam a piece of wood under his centre stand to stop his bike from wobbling. "Did the Police ever find your old Cub?"

"Police .... crap." Pete took off his battered old pudding basin helmet and ran his oily fingers through his equally oily hair. "Cecil found half in someone's front garden, and Graham found the other half being loaded into some one's van. Do you know what the Police said when we told 'em?" he screwed his face up in disgust, displaying in the process a beautiful set of broken teeth, "'Oh, ta. We knew it would turn up somewhere.' and they've had it in the nick as vital evidence ever since.

We'd have done better to have sorted it out ourselves."

"Hey look," Mick's voice had an edge of awe to it.

Everyone turned to see Cecil pull in on a gleaming 500cc B.S.A. Gold Star. It had all the goodies from clip-ons and alloy racing tank to lightened engine plates. He blipped the throttle so that the peasants could hear the exhaust twitter on the over run. "Out of the way Scum," Cecil pushed Pete's enquiring hand off the highly polished tank, "you might contaminate it!"

"What's this then? Where's the old Ducati then? Finally rusted away did it?" asked the dumbfounded Methanol Pete.

"No, 'corse not. It's just that this potent machine is more suitable for my great talents in road racing. Not that I couldn't get the best out of any machine" Cecil haughtily replied.

"Like when you turned my outfit over?" reminded Lew. Cecil ignored him and proceeded to put the wooden bung into the bell mouth of the down draught carburettor.

"Anyway, I thought I'd back Britain, and get a good old B.S.A." Cecil looked down and contemplated his left boot, "Mind you of course, the right hand gear change comes in handy, if you know what I mean."

"And they thought patriotism had died." Jesus and Isabel lead the others off towards the stadium.

"I'm putting a Gold Star silencer on my Velo," Big G confided to GR.

"What?"

"Yeh, I love that twitter. And then I'll get her repainted bright red."

GR hung his head over a fence.

"What's up with GR?" Gra asked as he fished behind his ear for the inevitable dog-end.

"Being sick I think."

The man on the Staff Stile looked up from his newspaper. "Hello boys; didn't think you were working tonight."

GR put his staff card and a complementary ticket on the counter. "Oh yes, we're working alright." GR gave Yvonne a squeeze.

"But not in the bars eh?" The old man winked, GR winked back. "Well you'd better cram two into the stile if you want to save your comp. tickets." The lads willingly complied and poured through into the stadium.

"Evening boys. You're not on tonight are you?" a voice boomed from the Catering Office.

"Evening Ted." GR, Lew, and the others who worked at the stadium part-time looked in. The cluttered office was in its usual chaotic state, beer bottles, hamburger buns, traveller's samples, and all sorts of other miscellaneous goods were heaped everywhere. Ted lent forward and offered a packet of un-tipped Senior Service cigarettes. The packet quickly emptied. The other two occupants of the office watched, and then laughed at Ted's expression.

Lew bent his head to accept the proffered light. "Nah, we're not working tonight, we're out for a nights entertainment."

"I can see that," Ted inclined his head towards GR and Yvonne who were entwined, and otherwise occupied. "Oh well, enjoy yourselves. But don't let me catch you conning drinks out of the bar or buffet girls."

"Girls," Foxy snorted as they moved back into the passageway, "most of 'em are old enough to be my grandmother."

In the office Bob smiled at the old man opposite him. "Things don't change much do they."

The old man flicked the ash off the end of his cigar, and smiled to himself. "Very true," he said in a cultured voice. "They may ride Hondas instead of Scotts, and Yamahas instead of Broughs, but they still get up to the same things as I," he waved his hand towards the others, "and indeed you, got up to."

110

Bob walked over to a half empty tin, took out a packet of biscuits, slit it open and commenced to eat them. "Yes, makes you feel young again just to remember."

Ted leaned back in his chair. "Hey, did I ever tell you about the time I took my old B.S.A. Gold Flash outfit down to ...."

The lads climbed the covered wooden terracing until they reached the very top.

"I thought we'd come here for entertainment, not exercise." Foxy, being short in the leg, was out of breath from trying to keep up with the others who had invariably taken the steps two at a time.

"Think yourself lucky, some of the track I've been to, " GR the speedway expert informed him, " have no cover whatsoever."

Scoffer sat down and sprawled over enough space for six. "Oh yes, 'corse they haven't. I suppose you'll be telling me next that when it rains they all get wet?"

"Yeh."

"Oh yeh, oh yeh. We know, we know."

The lads had just settled themselves down in the half empty stadium when a marching tune came over the loud speakers and the pushers and rakers came past, two by two.

"'ere, they are all out of step," complained Lew as he eased a baccy packet out of Gra's pocket.

GR broke away from what he was doing with Yvonne. "How much did you pay to get in?"

"Nothing."

"Then shut up."

The formalities were quickly over and the racing started. The two home riders were at the back and were trying to get past their opponents. The little old lady in front of the lads gave her rattle a hard twist that she did not appear capable of performing. "Get inside 'em, fence the bums, BRING 'EM

111

OFF."

"That's what I like about speedway," Lew proffered the baccy to GR, but seeing he was busy, passed it on to Foxy instead, "sportsmanship, and a nice family atmosphere."

The riders for the next race came out.

"Oi, Olly," a supporter hanging over the dog track yelled at the rider with the red crash helmet cover, "win this one, don't throw it!"

The rider, who was engaged in a deep conversation with the two riders from the other team, glanced over.

"Olly, MONEY!" yelled the home crowd. "Olly, MONEY!"

Olly poked two fingers at them and carried on talking.

"I don't reckon speedway much." Foxy put his boot into Lew's back, "Coming to the bar? I want ter drown me sorrows."

Lew nodded his assent and turned to ask Cecil if he wanted to come as well. Cecil was too busy, he had found two knotholes, and with only a little bit of discomfort, found that he could drop peanuts on the people in the buffet below through one hole and observe the results down the other.

"That's funny," Gra felt in his pockets, "I thought I'd brought me baccy with me. Must have left it at home."

"Here," Lew took the baccy pouch from Pete, "have this, it's almost empty, so you might as well keep the lot. You coming Foxy?"

Foxy formed his wad of chewing gum into a smooth pellet, rolled his tongue, aimed at the light-shade above his head, and blew. PHAT, DING. "No just finished." The two alcoholics headed off.

The speedway riders swooped round the track throwing their bikes into the bends and pulling big drifting wheel lockers.

"I used to do that sort of thing on my old Greeves," said Cecil.

"Yeh but they are doing it on purpose." Pete was not in a

very happy mood, a hole had just appeared in his tatty jumper and was spreading fast. Cecil looked elsewhere for a sympathetic ear. He nudged the lad sitting next to Pete.

"I used to do that sort of thing on my old Greeves. Dead easy it is."

Goosey, wearing a leather jacket, the newness of which was painfully obvious, was too engrossed in the racing to hear him. Cecil gave up, pulled out his packet of peanuts, and returned to the knotholes.

Gra pulled Sue towards him, "Come on luv." She pushed him away and continued to watch the racing. "Anyone would think we had come here to watch the speedway match," Gra protested to Jesus, but he was having too much of the same problem with Isabel to be sympathetic. "Honestly I don't know how you females can get so interested in that junk. You heard the bloke down the front, these races are all fixed. The winner is decided in the pits, not out on the track. There's not even any danger in it."

The leading rider got into too much of a drift on the bend in front of the lads and pulled a big locker. The rider behind cannoned into him. The two riders behind took evasive action, one missed the heap of men and machines. The other didn't. His machine and he parted company; the machine did a wheel-stand and then somersaulted over the fence onto the dog track; the rider shot into the wire safety fence and disappeared underneath it. The St. John's Ambulance men rushed to the spot and started carting off the bodies.

The lads gave up trying to divert the girl's attention to better things and settled down to watch the bikes. Even Yvonne had one eye open and on the track.

Eventually the meeting came to a close and the lads set off in search of Lew and Foxy. They found them weaving along the roadway beneath the stands, both trying to support the other,

113

and neither succeeding. Two lads took hold of each miscreant and frog marched them off to the bikes.

"You're too drunk to ride your own bike. I'd better take you home." Jesus pushed Lew into the coffin box that served for a sidecar. Isabel got in at the front and made sure Lew was facing downwind.

"Where's the car Foxy?" enquired Methanol Pete.

"Parshed away," Foxy slurred back. "You commin,'" he tried to focus on a septic pimple on Pete's nose, "you commin' to ver funeral?"

"Sure, sure. Do you want a lift?" Pete guided the inebriate lad towards the hencoop he called a sidecar.

Jesus turned to Goosey who stood watching Gra push his reluctant bike up and down the road in an attempt to start it. "It's just as well Foxy's drunk." Goosey turned with an uncomprehending look on his face. Jesus laughed and shook his well thatched head. "You obviously haven't had a lift from Pete. Well let's just say that the funeral on Friday night might not be just for L.T.2, but also for its master: Foxy!"

Chapter 10: BLACK IS BLACK

The lads stood quietly outside the Plough Road Baths, Battersea, as a lorry with L.T.2 in tow pulled into the side road. Big G jumped out of the cab and joined Foxy by the car. The lads formed a line facing L.T.2 whilst Foxy removed a few bits and pieces that might still be of use, and placed them in the back of the lorry next to an old piano.

Foxy turned and faced the congregation. "Dearly unwashed. We have gathered here tonight to say farewell to an old and faithful friend." He turned to face the car, picked up some gravel, and sprinkled it over the dented bonnet, "Ashes to ashes, dust to dust. If the big end don't get yer, the rust sure must." He bowed his head. Totter went over and removed the number plates whilst Cecil commenced removing the engine number with a file. The necessary removals having been completed Foxy came over to the lads and their girlfriends to thank them for their support in his time of need.

"You going home now then?" GR asked.

"Yeh. Big G has got to get the lorry back before his boss notices it's missing. Oh, but before that, we've got to drop the piano off. It's Goosey's birthday present."

GR looked surprised, "I didn't know Goosey played the piano."

"It ain't his birthday either!" Foxy leapt up onto the tail-board of the lorry, pulled up a box and sat in front of the piano. "And now we are going to play a waltz."

Plink plonk, plink plonk.

The lorry backfired and drove off into the night.

Chapter 11: COME ON BACK

Gra pushed past the Mods lounging round the entrance of the Joy Burger and headed for the table the lads were at, "'ere, Cecil's just been beaten up!"

The lads looked up. "What?" Foxy asked.

"You know that bird he tried to pick up? Well her boyfriend, brother, and a few others of the Henry Price Mob took offence and BANG!"

"That's it. It's the last straw." GR got up, "I'm off to the Bridge." He strode out of the door and a couple of others followed him out.

"Just cos him and his bird have split that GR's gone and got the sulks." Nutta shifted his generous posterior on the seat and returned to doodling in the spilt tea.

"No, GR's right. Mods, yobs, and us don't mix. We should stick to our own kind." Gurn went over, got his helmet from the helmet table, and left.

The others mulled the problem over.

"Perhaps, perhaps," Lew muttered.

GR, Cecil, and the others were warming their bikes up prior to leaving, when Big Ray pulled in. "Any of you lot coming up the Bridge?"

"That's for bleedin' real." Cecil carefully tried to put his goggles on over his swollen and puffed eye.

Big Ray looked around, "Anyone seen Sandy?"

GR indicated the Joy Burger, "She came with Foxy. Why?"

"Just let her know I'm here."

GR got off his bike, leaving it ticking over, and walked the entrance of the Joyburger and forced his way past the Mods who obviously thought that anywhere that sold hamburgers was their territory. GR caught Sandy's eye and pointed to Big Ray's bike outside. She got up and left. Foxy didn't notice her go; he was too busy describing the Humber Super Snipe he was thinking of buying as the replacement Lad Transporter.

The traffic was light and it didn't take long for the departing lads to reach the coffee stall at Chelsea Bridge. They had just got the steel plates they were sitting on warm when a Harley Davidson 750cc ex-US Army side-valve outfit and four outriders pulled in. The riders and the sidecar passenger undid a giant toolbox on the rear of the chair and started to work on the Harley's engine. Gurn looked at his watch, "They're late. They're usually here by nine."

"We ain't all regular," Goosey commented with a snigger.

Gurn put his arm round Goosey's neck, "Perhaps my friend, you ought to take senna pods."

A bus pulled into the stop opposite and a slight figure in a black leather jacket got off and crossed the road. Yvonne sat down next to GR. GR watched his boots and thought.

Alan, one of the lads from the Joy Burger, walked over to where the Big Feller and his mate Del were presiding over an enthusiastic court. "What's going on?" Alan pushed through to the front.

"What's going on you ask?" Del looked surprised. "Did you hear that? What's going on?"

The Big Feller smiled slowly; he was still trying to work out what was said the first time.

"This." With a sweep of his hand Del indicated an unusual looking motorbike and sidecar. "This is what is going on. Very much so."

Alan looked. The chair was conventional enough, a couple of planks of wood on a chassis with a car seat atop. But the bike was something else. It was not so much the bike really as the engine. The head and barrel on the Bonneville had been put on back to front. The straight through and straight running copper exhaust pipes made the bike look longer than it really was, whilst the forward facing carbs made it appear as if the engine was wearing glasses. Every possible piece of surplus metal had been removed; the alloy crankcase sides were dimpled in intricate circular patterns. Del smiled, "I drove me neighbours mad for a fortnight while I drilled that little lot."

Alan dragged his eyes away from the beastie, "Look like a bit of Swiss cheese."

"Bloody cheek. Makes it a lot lighter and," Del gave a sneering look in the direction of Alan's stock standard B.S.A. A65, embellished only by a dolphin faring, "faster."

"You're on." Alan went off to recruit a passenger.

"Any other takers?" Del challenged. "Down to the round-a-bout, back up, onto Sloane Square, and the finish line is the zebra crossing here." The other outfit owners went off to warm up their machines, all except the Harley rider. He and his escort were forming up to continue on their regular tour, and they didn't like their timetable interfered with.

"It's a shame Jesus isn't here to join in the fun." A clatter of worn tappets and clapped out big ends caught Pete's attention.

117

"Though talk of the Devil."

"How inappropriate," remarked Gurn.

"I thought I'd join you lot in exile." Jesus went to get off his bike.

"You're just in time for the sidecar race." Gurn pushed him back onto the bike.

Jesus laughed out loud, "What? On this?"

"Remember Totter at Boxhill," Pete reminded him as he poured some waste oil into the oil tank of his bike.

"Yeh, but Totter is mad. Anyway what am I going to do for a passenger?" Jesus indicated the coffin that Isabel had vacated some weeks back.

"Cecil's daft enough." Gurn pushed Cecil forward.

Jesus shook his head in disdain. "Not him. He'll be too busy after my arse to do any work."

"Well, he'll need to be over the saddle on the right handers anyway," Pete reminded him as the thick black oil glugged into his bike's cavernous oil tank.

Jesus went over to GR and Yvonne to see if he could persuade either of them to be his passenger. They were engrossed in looking at their boots, and failed to notice him. Jesus turned back to Cecil and, with a jerk of his oil stained thumb, indicated for him to get on board.

The outfits lined up across the road. A scarf came down and the eight machines leapt off the starting grid. Well seven leapt off; Jesus' outfit toddled off. The lads stood on the side supports of the Bridge to watch.

Despite all the laws of mechanics, Pete was in the lead, followed by Del and Alan, their passengers leaning over at ridiculous angles as they all power slid round the round-a-bout. Jesus was way behind everyone else and decided it was hopeless to try and stay in the race. Instead of going back up the Bridge after going round the round-a-bout he turned left into Battersea Park. Unfortunately he forgot to tell Cecil, who continued to hang over the saddle for the right hand curve of the round-a-bout. The law of centrifugal force prevailed and the weight transferred to the bike. With Cecil adding to the shifted weight rather than countering it, the plot turned turtle. The other sidecars pounded past the coffee stall, Del and Pete neck and neck. The blue haze from Pete's exhaust hung in the air.

"What about the lights? What if they are red?" a stranger to the Bridge asked.

"So? What if the lights are red? So?" The Big Feller couldn't understand why some one should ask such a silly question. "They've got a horn haven't they? They've even got good passengers haven't they? So what's the worry?"

Scoffer came along the road from the Chelsea side and pulled into the curb by the coffee staff. He was beaming like a Cheshire cat as he parked his newly acquired Norton Dominator at the end of the row of bikes and walked towards the lads. "Evening all. Guess what?"

Gurn broke off from his half eaten hot dog. "By the smile on your face; Norton have returned to racing."

"No, no, not quite as good as that. Leo has got the sack and the owners are reopening Bernie's at night again."

GR looked at Yvonne, "Do you want a lift home?" He held out his hand, she took it and they headed for his bike.

"Ain't that cute," said Cecil as he limped over.

"I'll give you cute." Jesus tweaked Cecil's ear. "You little bike wrecker you. You wait till I tell your mummy."

Scoffer looked over from the coffee stall where he was waiting for the decrepit owner to pour him some of the creosote tasting coffee "Cheer up Jesus, Bernie's is open again."

Chapter 12: LEADER OF THE PACK

The inside of Bernie's had been redecorated in bright orange for the grand reopening. Unfortunately the paint was cheap and already it was peeling off. A group of lads sat round a table industriously removing the new paint from the engravings. Pete had just removed the last speck from a Triumph emblem when Graham came in looking rather amused. "Anyone want to see some horse trading?"

"Oh well, it will help to pass the time." Lew removed his boots from the table and went outside, orange paint decorating the heels of his boots. Pete followed, vainly trying to find a pocket without a hole in it to put his knife into. There were quite a few lads outside watching with interest the antics of two gesticulating figures. "What's up?" Lew asked Cecil, who seemed completely absorbed in the spectacle.

"Eh?" Cecil gave a start. "Oh, well, Big G fancies Goosey's outfit and is making an offer."

"What's he offered?" Lew ran the fag he had just rolled along his tongue and was about to put it in his mouth when Gra took it and put it in his own mouth. Lew started to roll another.

"Who?"

"Big G."

"Oh, his Velo." Lew had almost got his fag into his mouth when Cecil, almost absently, took it from him. Lew started to roll yet another. "What's all the haggling? Hasn't Goosey offered enough cash on top then?"

"You've got it all wrong my lad." Cecil struck a red headed match on the wall and lit his roll up. "It ain't Goosey who's got to up the offer, it's Big G. Goosey's sticking out for all the original Velo equipment to go with it, silencer and all."

"Eh?" Lew quickly put his freshly rolled fag into his mouth to prevent it being stolen, and returned the baccy pouch to his pocket.

Pete joined them and removed Lew's baccy pouch from it's hiding place. He rolled a skinny fag. "Cecil, you work at

Eelights, you're in the trade. How much is Big G's Velo worth?'"

"Twenty five quid if he just sold it, forty if he traded it in. Mind that's Eelights price, Commerfords would probably give you a bit more."

Pete pulled his eyes from Goosey and Big G who seemed at last to have come to an agreement, "Goosey only paid a fiver for that bike."

Lew put his arm round Pete's shoulder and guided him back to the café. "As I was saying to Goosey at the synagogue only last Saturday, 'Goosey, my boy ....'".

Gra nudged Jesus who was chuckling to himself, "I thought you said that Goosey would never make a lad?"

Jesus inclined his head, "Perhaps, perhaps." They followed Lew and Pete back into the steamy interior of Bernie's.

"Hello der bawana, how's you gettin' on tonight den?"

Lew gave the lad beside him at the counter a patronising look, "If you keep on like that Rastus, one day your skin will turn black."

Rastus rolled his eyes and waved his hands in the air in best 'Black and White Minstrels' manner, "Holy Mackrel." He turned to the Greek who was serving him "Hey, white trash; you make sure dat my coffee is nice and black; eh man?"

Lew carved his way through the throng and returned to his seat in the rear room of the cafe, "All that bloke needs is a tin of boot polish on his face and he could get through Brixton without a passport," he said to no one in particular. He spotted GR, who not had not long arrived. "Hey GR. Did you hear about Nutta?" GR wasn't really interested. He was trying to prevent the game of table football he was playing from turning into a whitewash. "Yeh," Lew continued, "suffering from a broken heart he is. His girlfriend up and left him, just like that. They'd been going out for over a year too."

GR conceded the last goal, and returned to the table looking dejected. "So what. What's new about that?"

Gurn looked up from polishing his glasses, "Always the same when you go out with schoolgirls. First week theys are at work they finds they can pick blokes up without any trouble." He 'hurred' on the lenses and continued polishing them. "They finds that they can get blokes that hasn't always got grease and dirt under their fingernails, and who hasn't always got their hands in theys holey pocket paying for bike repairs. Blokes that's got cars. Blokes what don't gets them soaked every time it rains, nor gets them frozen every winter." He replaced his glasses. "Still we do have better luck comes summer!"

Yvonne came over with two cups of tea in her hands; the slops dripped down the sides of the cracked cups and plopped onto the floor. She looked rather excited. "Hey, everyone is going up the 59 Club."

GR took the proffered cup without looking up. "I don't know if I fancy it tonight. All that traffic and all."

Yvonne looked hurt, "Oh come on. I'm sure you don't want me to go and cadge a lift off some one else. Do you?"

"Ok, ok," he turned and studied Lew and Gurn's faces. "Hmmmm."

Lew headed for the side door, "If we're off I'd better go and have a Jimmy." He open the door, went into the yard, and joined the long queue that stretched to the bog house door.

"Why don't you do it in the bloke in front's pocket?" Lew asked Moonie who was watching with interest the antics of Cecil who was searching for something in the garden; a couple of dock leaves in his hand.

"Eh?"

"Why don't you do it in the bloke in front's pocket?" repeated Lew.

"He'd notice."

"You didn't when I did it in yours."

Moonie didn't believe him for one moment, but felt in his

pocket all the same.

"What's the hold up?" Totter enquired of the lad at the head of the queue.

"Two birds in there," the lad nodded towards the dingy lean-to alongside him. "You know what birds are like when they get in there."

Totter tried the door but found it was locked. He went round to a small grime encrusted window, shook it, and pulled it open "Oi."

One girl was on the seat, the other stood with her back to the door effectively blocking the knotholes. They looked over shocked.

Totter stuck his head in, "Oi, you, Cheeky." The girl on the seat went a deep shade of scarlet. "Can you swim? I hope so 'cos if you don't hurry up we will all have to do it outside and flood the place," he withdrew his head and closed the window.

After much scuttling, two red faced girls emerged from the bog and hurried back into the cafe.

"After you," the lad at the head of the queue waved Totter in. "In consideration of your great work for mankind."

GR and Yvonne looked up as the side door slammed and two females rushed through the café. "Now if they had been two little boys, I'd have said Cecil was outside."

The door opened again and this time it was indeed Cecil who rushed in, followed by an irate Graham brandishing a handful of dock leaves.

"That's funny. I wonder what that's all about?" asked Yvonne.

Pete pushed the ashtray in front of him across the table, causing it to spill its contents on the way. "Didn't you hear what happened to Gra?" He studied the faces of the lads round the table, seeing that none of them had, he continued his story, "Well you know that bird he's been taking out?"

Gurn scratched his head as he tried to think. "You mean

123

Fred?"

"Yes Fred. Well it would appear that Gra took her courting last week. He started to get up to his usual tricks when," Pete paused and swallowed a mouthful of stone cold tea and grimaced as it hit his stomach, "when, due to inaccuracy on his part, or with malice afore-thought on her part, he had sexual intercourse with a bunch of stinging nettles."

Gurn winced. GR smirked and leant forward, "I'd better tell the Pope of that one. It might be an acceptable form of contraception."

Everyone laughed, except Yvonne.

The ride to the 59 Club was, apart from a couple of dices along Hyde Park, uneventful and the lads parked their machines in the fenced area at the front of a majestic Church. The Church grounds were packed with hundreds of bikes, streetlights reflected off the polished surfaces of the machines making the whole glitter.

Two motorcycles approached. The lead machine was a Yamaha and it pulled up in a haze of blue smoke, the marshal at the gate saw the 59 badge on the fly screen and waved him on. The second machine arrived seconds later, it was a Police Triumph Saint. The rider tried to follow the other motorcycle into the grounds, but the marshal blocked the way. The head marshal approached the rider. "Where's your club card?"

The Policeman looked up "Eh?"

"You can't come in here unless you are a member."

"I'm the Law!"

"How do we know? There are that many ex-Police bikes around, half the club is on them. I think I'd better see your Warrant Card."

The Policeman went to ride through but he was now surrounded by more than a dozen marshals and a couple of dozen spectators. He fished in his pocket and pulled out his card. The head marshal examined it minutely. A gate clanged at the rear of the Churchyard and a two- stroke could be heard moving off at a rapid rate of knots. The marshal gave back the Warrant Card. "Sorry about that Officer, we can't be too careful you know. You can go through now."

The Policeman bit his lip and backed his motorcycle into the road. He pulled off in the direction of the rear entrance.

"Nice to belong to a club that looks after its member's interests," said Lew as they waited for GR. GR was having difficulty in getting the ignition key out of his bike, he gave up and came over to where the others were standing. They crossed the road and approached the Clubhouse. After much flourishing of cards and passing over of money, they went in. The downstairs of the converted schoolhouse was a lot cleaner than the usual haunts of the lads. The walls were brightly painted brick, and the fact the paint had been donated meant that no two walls were the same colour. In fact some walls were two or even three different colours. The lads went over to a small room and handed in their helmets and gloves at the helmet park. It was a warm evening so the lads didn't bother buying any tea or hot food from the buffet but, instead, went straight upstairs, taking their jackets off as they went.

Most of the lads headed for the football and pin-tables, a few settled down on the rickety chairs and thumbed through the old magazines that covered the tables. Yvonne was going to put some records on the jukebox, but the noise from the crowed hall drowned the music that was already on. She changed her mind and headed instead for the stage where a large selection of motorcycle clothing and badges were being offered for sale. Gra tried to pinch her arse as she went by, but she was too quick for him.

GR pulled Gra off his seat and stuffed him against the wall. "You after my bird?"

"No, no."

GR relaxed his grip, then forced Gra against the wall again. "You saying there's summat wrong with her?"

"No, no."

GR let Gra go, then grabbed hold of him again. "So, you are after her!"

Gra got the giggles, "No, no. Honest I ain't."

GR relaxed his grip, but before Gra could get away he found himself against the wall yet again. "So, you do think there's summat wrong with her!"

Gra was laughing so much that if GR hadn't got hold of him he'd have been rolling on the floor. "No," tears welled in Gra's eyes, "no."

GR was just going to shove his mate against the wall for the fifth time when the game was interrupted by the appearance of two men with grey thinning hair. One wore a leather jacket and jeans and a black dog collar, the other was more conventionally dressed, the purple of his own dog collar contrasting with his light grey suit.

"Hello lads," said the Reverends Bill Shergold. "Behaving yourselves?" He waited for the banter to finish, "And how are you Cecil? Getting on all right without your toe? Good." He continued to escort the man in the light grey suit around the club.

"As you can see Bishop," they eased their way through the crowd by the jukebox, "we provide many facilities for these lads, but it is essential that the Church continues to give us support. Otherwise we may run into financial difficulties again."

The Bishop nodded his head in agreement as they waded back to the exit by the stage. He pushed himself plush against the wall as two lads pushed past and chased each other down the stairs. "It's a shame though Bill that you can't get some of the other youngsters here. You know, the 'Mods'. After all, the 59 Club was originally an ordinary Youth Club, not just a motorcycle club."

Bill looked over his flock. "As you know we don't preach to the lads, and we don't try to cram religion down their throats. However, by example, understanding, and," he gave a little smile, "by bringing Christian attitudes and views to them, we have found that most are willing to consider, even if they don't always seem to adopt, a more Christian way of life. Loving their Mod neighbour is, however, one principle they will not take to."

The Bishop watched as Bill put a finger behind the grubby and oil marked dog collar he was wearing and wiped away the sweat "These Rockers of yours, they can't just go on living in a state of constant war. The Mods far out number them, and they won't just go away."

Bill took out a handkerchief and wiped his brow. "That's just it Bishop, they will," he put the handkerchief back in his pocket. "You see Mods are fashion, and fashions change."

The Bishop studied the crammed hall, and fingered his lip speculatively. "Even so Bill, surely you can appeal to the different gang leaders to stop all the trouble there has been? Surely they could do it if they wanted to?"

Bill chuckled, "I'm afraid Bishop you've been reading too many magazines, and watching too many American films. There are no gang leaders; there aren't any real gangs. These lads live in a kaleidoscope society. Sometimes here; sometimes there. Sometimes riding with this crowd; sometimes with that crowd. Question them about their riding companions and few will be able to give you their names, or if they do, it will only be a nickname. It is these things that what make it their society so resilient."

Yvonne came off the stage and admired the white silk scarf she had just bought. She caught Bill and the bishop watching her, they smiled, she smiled back and went to join GR.

GR got up and put his Honda handbook back into his jacket

pocket. "Come on luv, I want you." He held out his hand to Yvonne and they left.

Cecil nudged Foxy in the ribs causing him to spill his baccy. Foxy rummaged on the floor to try and retrieve as much of the precious weed as he could. "Alright Ces, what up? Someone bending over or summat?"

Cecil pointed to GR and Yvonne as they went down the stairs hand-in-hand "I bet I know where they are going and what they are going to get up to!" He gave a lecherous laugh and bent down to help Foxy gather up his baccy, collecting enough in the process to roll himself a couple of cigars.

The bikes were close packed and Yvonne had great difficulty in the restricted space keeping the torch beam on the side of the bike where GR had dismantled his broken ignition switch. He was trying to short-circuit the wiring so that they would be able to get home that night.

Chapter 13: RUNAWAY

A little fat boy jumped up and down on the pavement and gestured wildly as a gaggle of about fifty Mods on scooters rode past. "Yah, stinking Mods. Come over here and let us sort yer out!" He poked two fingers at them, "Arse 'ole bandits, mummies boys, chickens. Go suck on yer Wimpies!"

"Oi, Pete." Foxy inclined his head towards the boy, who was now throwing empty drink cans after the disappearing scooters, "Can't you do nothing with your little brother?"

Pete wiped the dirty oil off of his hands onto his jeans, "He's only twelve."

"Stones or tons?"

"Nah years old. He don't mean no harm."

Foxy put his hands in his trouser pockets and rocked on his heels, "If you don't shut him up he won't live to be thirteen;

stones, tons, or years." He pointed up to where the Mods were doing a U-turn and coming back. "And it don't look too promising for us neither."

Pete grabbed his brother and dragged him into the cafe.

"Does he bite?" Lew watched as Pete tried to contain the youngster, finally succeeding with a full Nelson.

"This, I regret to say, is my little," Pete waited for the laughing to stop, "my little brother; Jim."

"Har, har, Jim lad. Take yer 'ands off me crutch." Cecil hobbled on one leg over to the jukebox and commenced to shove foreign coins in.

"Well Jim lad," Lew tweaked the restrained boy's ear, "you'd better behave yourself or we will give you to Cecil to play with."

"Oh no you won't, you peasant," Cecil started a hasty retreat to the other end of the cafe. "I'm a sadist, not a masochist."

"Come on you," Pete let his brother go and indicated a seat. "Move." He assisted the boy on his way with the toe of his boot. "What's up with GR?"

GR sat watching his tea. Yvonne sat watching GR.

Foxy cleaned his fingernails with a small screwdriver. "Well you know that accident he had when he hit that old bloke? Well the old codger went and died last night. That's probably it."

"Nah, its female trouble if you ask me." Lew rummaged in his back pocket for a dog-end of smokeable length. "It's his own fault. He ought to spend more time on his bike, and less time chasing girls."

"Sour grapes." Totter pushed past. Lew ignored him and lit his small dog-end, being very careful not to burn his nose with the ether smelling lighter.

"His trouble is," Gra downed his cup of tea in one gulp, "he thinks too much. Thinking only makes you unhappy."

Lew took a deep draw on his fag then dropped it into the ashtray when it burned his finger. "So, that's why you are such

129

a bundle of fun, is it?"

Moonie came over with Jacky in tow, "Doing anything tonight?"

Cecil stopped selecting tunes on the jukebox and turned round "Why? Do you fancy me then?"

"Credit me with some taste. No actually a couple of the lads from Tooting Arcade got worked over by Mods last week. At a club in Belleview Road. They thought we might like to go a visiting."

"What, violence?" Lew looked shocked.

"It's something to do. Anyway I don't suppose anything will come of it."

Jesus started to put on his helmet, "Come on, it will make a change."

Lew went over to GR who was still studying his tea. Lew smiled sympathetically to Yvonne. "Oi, GR. Are you coming?"

"Eh? What?"

Lew picked up GR's helmet from the helmet table and gave it to him. "We're going for a ride, you're coming."

GR got up and followed. Yvonne held out her hand, but GR didn't seem to see it, she shrugged and tagged on behind doing up her helmet as she went.

GR aimed the rifle, steadied himself and gently squeezed the trigger. BANG. The target went out. He straightened up and took the sixpence Yvonne had retrieved from the return slot of the machine. He was just going to put it back in for another round when Moonie and Little Ray came over.

"Enjoying yerself?" Little Ray drew pictures on the glass front of the machine with a wetted finger.

"Half an hour, and it ain't cost me a penny."

"Quite a little Wyatt Twerp, ain't you." Little Ray gave Yvonne a wink; she looked the other way. "Well you won't have time for any more. We're off," he pushed his way to the exit.

"That's funny." GR looked around. "Lew said we were going for a ride, most of the Arcade Mob are heading for the Underground station."

Jesus came alongside buckling up his helmet as he walked "You know the trouble with you GR is that you think too much."

"Some ride," GR looked across at the Church hall opposite the side road where the lads sat on their parked bikes. "Some ride," he put his hand on the Honda's engine. "Didn't even get the oil warm."

"Well," Moonie broke away from a passionate necking session he and Jacky were having, "well we thought we'd go to a Youth Club dance instead. Make a change like."

"You don't like dancing," GR accused Moonie.

"Hey look, here come the others." Lew who had been keeping watch down the main road, turned back to face the lads. "And guess who's leading them GR? Spinx and," Lew paused for effect, "Johnny France. I haven't seen him since he was chucked out of school."

"Did you say Johnny France?" GR buried his head in his hands. "Johnny France. Just what sort of trouble are you lot getting me into?"

"Come on," Jesus helped Foxy to dismount from the outfit. "And don't bother locking the bikes. We might need them in a hurry," he gave a wicked laugh and checked the adjustable spanner was still in his jeans back pocket.

With a roar and a twitter Cecil pulled in and parked his Goldie at the end of the row of bikes. "Hello peasants. Ready for the dance are we?" Cecil dismounted and trolled towards where the Arcade Mob we milling around outside the Youth Club. The others followed him.

"Not being men of violence," Lew addressed his colleagues

from Bernie's, "I feel it would be prudent if we went in last, so that, whilst we give psychological assistance by building up the numbers, we will, in fact, be ideally placed to make a strategic withdrawal if the situation deteriorates."

Gra elbowed Foxy, who was practising fierce looks, "What's all that mean?"

Foxy looked up at him, "We stick at the back, then if things get rough, we can piss off quick. Give us a fag Gra."

Graham obliged and the lads watched as Johnny France gave the doorman a shove and the lads from the Tooting Arcade moved into the hall.

"Hey Prefect. You still pushing your weight around?"

GR turned and studied the short youth with cropped hair and dressed in a Mod fashion that had been out of date for at least two months. "I thought you'd have been in Borstal by now. Must be at least three years since we got you flogged for running the third year Mafia protection racket." GR and Yvonne moved to one side in order to let the Bernie's crowd enter the hall.

"Nah." The old fashioned Mod studied the packet of cigarettes in his hand, "I won't be sent to Borstal. I'm too cunning these days."

"Tell me," GR took a proffered cigarette and passed it onto Yvonne, "do you ever see anything of that fellow with the limp? The one that stank to high heaven .... "

The inside of the hall was dark and the lads stayed in a group to help maintain the appearance of strength. Johnny France and Spinx strolled down one side examining faces and knocking over tables. They stopped at the end table. Johnny France drew himself up to his full six foot six inches and glared down at the dozen or so Mods seated below him. "I believe you have been naughty boys, and I think that you ought to know that my friends here," he indicated the mob of lads at the other end of the hall, "think that you need your botties smacked."

The Mods pushed away their chairs and stood up. The lads walked slowly and deliberately down the hall towards them.

"Oi!" GR poked his head through the door. "Law. A Noddy bike has just pulled in."

The lads stopped in their tracks.

"What's one Noddy bike?" one of the birds from the Arcade asked as she cracked her knuckles in anticipation of a decent fight.

"No, he's right." Moonie turned back for the door, "There may only be one here now, but in a few minutes they will be swarming around here like flies round shit."

The lads followed Moonie out and congregated on the corner opposite the Church hall.

First the squad cars arrived, three or four of them, then the meat wagons arrived and disgorged their blue clad contents, and then two dog vans arrived followed by a motorcycle patrol.

"Won't they be disappointed when they find that the cupboard is bare," Little Ray led the others back to the bikes. "Still it wasn't a waste really. The Mods got a fright, the reputation wasn't put to the test, and we found out how long it takes to get from Tooting nick to Belleview Road."

"Well, what now?" Lew asked. The lads looked at each other.

"I know," Moonie was full of ideas that night, "GR wants to go for a ride. Lew's always boasting about what that pre-war camel of his will do. Why don't we put the two together? We'll go down to Garrett Lane and Lew and Graham can see just what the Velo will do. We can follow behind and pace them."

Jesus looked over from where he was trying to tie his front number plate back on "What about me and Foxy? This old bus won't do sixty, let alone the eighty Lew claims he can do."

Moonie had thought of everything, he was in an organising mood. "Drop the outfit off at Lew's place and Little Ray and Cecil can give you two a pillion ride."

They all looked at Lew "Ok, I'll show you just how they built bikes in the good old days." Lew mounted up and booted the Velo into life.

The sat at the Earlsfield lights facing towards Tooting, there were no more traffic lights for three miles, and the road surface was just made for racing on. Lew, with Graham in the chair, were alone on the front grid. The solos, two by two, were behind, well spread over the road to prevent interference.

"Oi," Cecil turned to Foxy who was squeezed up on the none too generous space Cecil had left him on the end of the skimpy racing saddle. "Don't rape me every time I go over a bump."

Foxy grimaced and continued to search around the saddle for a non-existent handhold "You should be so lucky. I'll be too busy trying to hang on to be worrying about the pleasures of the flesh."

The lights changed and the bikes pulled off sharply.

The first bend was a long sweeping right hander and Lew didn't have to shut off for it. He pulled the bars round and pointed the front wheel at the exit. The back drifted slightly. Gra put a bit more weight over the saddle to help keep traction. Now the straight, Gra lay down inside the bare interior of the chair keeping just the top of his head in the slipstream. Cars, cars, everywhere, they knew that they wouldn't get a good run if this kept up. The outfit and its escort thundered on.

The Sommerstown S-bends loomed up. Gra gripped the old fan belt Lew had attached to the sidecar's chassis and lent over the chair's wheel as best he could. The old fashioned chassis had a large diameter wheel, thus preventing Gra from doing any real tarmac scraping. Quickly, and without any jolting movement Gra pulled himself back and hung out over the saddle as Lew changed to the opposite lock and blasted them round the tight right hander; more cars. It took them until Eelights to weave past the traffic and they had no chance to open up again before the kink in the road at Tooting. Lew saw that there was no traffic coming the other way and cut a straight line across. Fortunately Gra, being a good passenger, read Lew's thoughts and acted correctly.

The bikes did a U-turn by the lights. Moonie conferred with the others as they dawdled along the road. He then came alongside Lew, "Sixty five, and no more."

"Too much traffic. I'll see if I can get a better run on the way back." Lew gunned the bike forward and Moonie and the other solos dropped back to follow.

There was little traffic and they were going quite well. Just as he came into the final bend Lew saw the needle speedo tremble between seventy five and eighty. Gra lent over the chair wheel as they drifted round the bend, despite all efforts the chair refused to stay on the road. Lew saw the lights ahead of them change to green. He knew the timing of the lights and that he wouldn't get through them. He shut off and started to go down the gears as the bike slowed. Five hundred yards and the lights were still green. Down into second. Lew decided to chance it for, if he carried on down the Lane and got onto the long straight into Wandsworth, he might yet get the dead eighty. Three hundred yards, still green. Lew gunned it. He twisted the throttle wide open and sent the needle on the taco up to eight thousand. The lights changed to red. The pathetic brakes on the old Velo struggled to cope, but obviously were not going to stop the outfit on their own. In a fraction of a second Lew thought of all the possible solutions to the problem, including jumping the lights, and settled for the least dangerous. He blipped the throttle and dropped into first gear. The back wheel bit into the road with a squeal, the taco needle went off the clock .... BANG.

The only sound anyone was conscious of, as the crippled outfit rolled into the curb the other side of the lights, was the sound of the chain going round.

Chapter 14 HE'S IN TOWN

Cecil and Gurn pulled into the space in front of the coffee stall on the Bridge, two Policemen indicated that the lads were to remain seated. Gurn gave Cecil a quizzical look. Cecil just shrugged.

One of the Policemen came over, "Nah then, sonny. What's the registration number of the bike what you are riding?"

Gurn gave the correct answer. The Policeman looked disappointed and went on to check the Road Tax disc. That too was correct and he went off to question Cecil. Gurn started the big Triumph up and returned to the round-a-bout at the bottom of the road. The least he could do was to try and warn the others.

Cecil passed the grilling and went over to the coffee stall and purchased some of the noxious fluid. The Big Feller was propping up the none too clean counter with his none too clean body. "What's going on?" Cecil asked him.

The Big Feller let the question soak into his brain. After a minute or so gave his considered opinion, "Fings are a bit confused tonight." He massaged his face for a while whilst he gathered his thoughts. "See, the Mods tried to take over the Bridge earlier. Seems like they don't like us invading the Park and wanted to get their own back."

Cecil took a mouthful of coffee and swallowed it before the revolting flavour could make itself apparent. "Well what did they expect? There ain't so many of them as there were, not like a couple of years ago. But trying to take over the Bridge!" he shook his head in disbelief. "The lads will want revenge for that."

The Big Feller frowned uncomprehendingly.

"Get their own back," Cecil explained.

The Big Feller smiled, "Oh. They've been doing that already. That's why the Law is floating around."

Some more lads from Bernie's pulled in with Gurn bringing up the rear. After they had passed through the Gestapo, Cecil went and explained to them what had happened. Del, accompanied by a lad in leather jeans came over too. "Any of you lot fancy a ride in the Park? We are planning a little excursion."

"Shame GR ain't here. He likes cutting up scooters." Gra buckled up his helmet and pulled on his gloves. "Rather warped that way he is."

Little Ray shook the tank of his bike and looked through the filler hole to check the fuel situation. "Aye, well, its little wonder really. He got set upon by a dozen or so quite a while back. Outside the Fish and Chip shop, other end of Garrett Lane, by Burntwood Lane." Satisfied that he had enough juice for the excursion and the return home, Little Ray put the petrol cap back on. "Now he sits up there for hours on his bike waiting for them to come by so that he can play with them."

"At the Fish and Chip shop, the other end of Garrett Lane? That's bad, really bad. That's supposed to be neutral territory." Gra shook his head in disbelief.

The lads restarted their bikes and tagged onto the end of the file of motorcycles entering the Park.

Two dozen bikes in Indian file poodled along following a gaggle of scooters that were sprawled all over the road in front, like spilt paint. One by one the bikes pounced, cutting and weaving as they went. As the last bike completed the manoeuvre the rest roared off along the narrow lane, leaving the shattered Mods far behind. The bikes slowed down again. Then they came across another gaggle, and repeated the exercise. A third gaggle loomed in front. The lead bike was about to start the fun, when a motorcycle coming the opposite way started flashing his headlight. The lead bike dropped back. GR stopped flashing, took his hands off of the handlebars and waved the lads down. As they came round the next bend in the narrow road the lads saw what the trouble was. A dozen or so Police motorbikes were parked under the trees, riders with helmets on, engines running, ready for action. The lads did a careful U-turn, waved to the nice Policemen, and returned to the Bridge.

When they got there, they found that Pete had arrived and was emptying a half-gallon of waste oil into his bottomless oil tank. Little Ray went over to him, "Just had some fun with the Mods in the Park," he said. "We could have done with your dispensable outfit. It would have lent a little bit of weight." He watched as Pete threw the now empty can into the chair, "GR saved us from a nicking."

Pete showed little interest. He took off his gloves, the side of his right hand was covered in fresh blood. Pete watched with fascination as the blood trickled down his fingers, the bright red contrasting with the black oil. "A lot of traffic around tonight."

Little Ray looked at the paint marks on Pete's chair, and then at Pete, "The trouble with you Methanol Pete is that you can't remember that you are on a combo, not a solo." Little Ray looked over at the crowd by the stall. " Ah, there's GR. I must go and give him a pat on the back. Bye the bye, who's that with him?"

Cecil, who had just joined the pair, put on a knowing look, "That's his new girlfriend."

Little Ray sat on the seat of Pete's bike to observe the object of their discussion, then realising how dirty the seat was, got up quickly. "I wonder how long it will be before him and Yvonne get back together? I think she's still keen on him."

Cecil removed a battered Gaulois cigarette from his pocket and, after fighting off Gra and Pete, lit it. "This one must be keen on him too. Did you hear about the first time he took her out?" Nobody had, and nobody was interested, but he continued to flaunt his knowledge, "Well not only did he take her to that most romantic of shows, the Brighton Motorcycle Show, he took her on the only day it rained. And," he blew a cloud of foul smelling smoke over the others, "and, not only did it rain, he decided to indulge in some high speed dices with some of the lads, on Jap tyres too. When he took her home, he got lost. She had to finish the trip by train, whilst he tried to find his way through the back streets of Addington to get home to his mummy and daddy." Cecil finished with a flourish of his hand, and flicked cigarette ash onto Pete's hair.

"And she's still going out with him?" Pete rubbed the ash in and watched the couple as they made their way over to the side of the Bridge. "She must be keen."

"Or soft in the head?" suggested Little Ray as he discreetly picked black bits out of his eyes.

"Wrong, wrong. This time it's GR that's doing the chasing," informed the all knowing Cecil.

The lads went over to inspect GR's new girlfriend. "Evening GR, evening luv," Little Ray tried for starters.

The girl nodded her head in acknowledgement and engrossed herself in drinking her tea, her fair hair shrouding her face. Gra pulled his eyes off her and addressed himself to GR who was yakking to Cecil and Pete.

"Hey GR. Did you hear about Devon?" Gra asked as he rummaged in his pocket for his crumpled packet of tobacco.

GR turned and faced Gra, who was now trying to roll a fag from insufficient baccy, it being the day before pay-day. "No. Why?"

"Seems the Night Prowler put a bun in her oven, and then vanished."

"Night Prowler eh?" Scoffer jumped down from the steel bridge support and joined the others. "Doesn't surprise me. I remember how he came up the Saltbox one night with me and a couple of others. Carved us all up at high speed, and then buggered off. Anyone who does that sort of trick to his mates

139

ain't to be trusted."

GR took off his helmet and put it on the steel casement of the bridge, "I remember Devon alright. She was going out with Big G for a while and I did him a favour by carting her mate everywhere. Right dragon she was too, looked like a witch."

Cecil put his Gaulois on the encasement while he blew his nose. Gra picked up the fag and commenced to smoke it. "She was friendly though wasn't she. Bet she saw you alright."

GR smiled, "You're joking. Kellogs may give you toy cowboys with their Cornflakes, but it wouldn't have been toy cowboys that she'd have given me!"

Gra was amused, he looked at GR's new girlfriend for her reaction, but her long hair veiled her face and thoughts. Disappointed he looked away. A strange sight pulling in from across the road caught his eye. "Oh, err," he stammered, "look over there, here comes Lew." The others looked, but couldn't believe their eyes. Lew was back on the old James. It was as if the last six months hadn't been. "When did you get it back?" the lads crowded round.

"This evening. You know that bloke at work I sold it to for ten pounds? Well he only did about ten miles on it before it packed up. Been in a shed ever since." Lew pulled the ancient bike onto its centre stand, pulled a wedge of wood from his jacket pocket, and stuck the wedge under one of the stand legs to keep it on an even keel. "I gave him a fiver for it, which was fair as it was a non-runner, spent five minutes tinkering with the points, and here I am. You should have seen his face when it started up!"

Big Ray tapped Lew on the shoulder, "Want to buy a new set of bars?" Big Ray pointed to his bike that sported a pair of scrambles bars plus a pair of clip-ons underneath. The prospective buyer went over to inspect the merchandise.

Moonie sat on the Bridge behind Big Ray's bike, "You make sure them clip-ons are done up tight Ray. Nasty things can happen if they ain't." Moonie rubbed the stub of what had been a thumb on his jeans in an attempt to revive the circulation in the amputated member.

"Talking of nasty things," the lad in leather jeans standing on the Bridge's steel encasement said," I can see a couple of traffic cops, and they are headed this way."

As usual, those with no Road Tax, Driving Licences, or parking lights left in a hurry for the Park, the others switched on their lights, and waited. The cops pulled in and commenced to check the bikes.

One came over to Gra, "I saw you in the Park earlier my lad. It's just as well you slowed down when you did, or you'd 'ave been in trouble. We're keeping an eye on you lot, so behave yerselves."

Goosey approached the Policeman's bike and pulled off the spark plug suppresser. It was of the two piece type. Goosey pulled it apart, removed the contact, put it back together, and replaced it on the spark plug. He walked round to the other side and did the same.

The second Policeman came over just as Goosey had finished. "Who owns that decrepit James over there?"

Lew looked up from the fag he was rolling, "Me. Why?"

"Your lights are so dim, you'd be better off with a candle."

Voices were cleared.

"All the nice girls love a candle," sang Gra.

All the lads on the Bridge joined in:

"All the nice girls love a wick,

For there's something about a candle,

That reminds them of a ...."

"Do you lot want me to book you all for obscene language?" asked the second copper who looked very annoyed.

Goosey went over to his Police bike and turned the petrol off.

The second Policeman continued to threaten and lecture the lads ".... and finally; if you lot give us any more trouble we are going to clear you off the Bridge for obstruction." He went over to his machine and waited for his companion to start his bike up. The first Policeman bounced up and down on the kick-start, his face getting redder and redder. Nothing happened. He flooded the carb, cleared the clutch, took it over compression, and swung on the kick-start. Still nothing happened. He lost his temper and commenced to pump the kick-start until he got too out of breath. The lads gave him vocal encouragement.

"Perhaps you've forgotten to wind it up," Lew offered helpfully.

"Nah, you've got to put cheese in those Mickey Mouse things!" Gra added for his twopenn'th.

"Oi, Sandy. Take the elastic out of yer knickers. The rubber band 'as broken in this gentlemen's engine," Little Ray called across. Sandy gave him the British worker's two finger salute.

The Policeman finally gave up, exhausted. He called on his R.T. for a breakdown truck. After some time it arrived, the lads helped to put the bike in the back, acquiring a few useful bits and pieces in the process. The truck pulled off and the remaining traffic cop started his bike and followed. It went about a quarter of a mile before the petrol in the carb ran out and the bike stopped accompanied by jeers from the lads.

Gra put his chin on Jesus' shoulder, being careful to avoid Jesus' flowing and pristine clean locks, "You know, you did underestimate Goosey. I think he has all the makings of a first class lad."

Jesus shook Gra's head off his shoulder, and flicked imaginary fleas off of his jacket, "I hate to admit it, particularly to a bum like you, but I think you could, only could mind, could be right."

The disappearance of the Police allowed the runaways to sneak back to the Bridge from their hiding place in the Park. They had not long returned when a Triumph Bonnie arrived and pulled into a vacant space. The rider and his pillion got off.

Rastus went for the teas whilst Yvonne walked over and sat on the bridge support to watch GR and his new girlfriend.

"Who's that?" the new girlfriend asked.

"Eh? Oh, just an old friend." GR lifted his hand to Yvonne in recognition.

Rastus came back with the teas and sat down next to Yvonne, his back to GR and the girl. Yvonne pulled Rastus towards her and commenced to give him a passionate kiss. He needed no encouragement and responded willingly. Yvonne's eyes were on GR; GR shook his head slowly and took his new girlfriend's hand. Tears welled in Yvonne's eyes and she broke her mouth away from Rastus' and hid her head in his shoulder, her hair falling forward, hiding her face.

Chapter 15: I UNDERSTAND

The wet road glistened and sparkled in the cold night air, Cecil looked appraisingly at it and snorted, his breath hanging suspended. A crowd of lads milled around wiping saddles, adjusting helmets, or fiddling with the bikes.

Slowly the machines were started up. Cecil went and joined Gurn and Pete who were sitting on the steel encasement of the Bridge. "Did you hear about GR and his new girl?" he asked.

Pete wasn't really interested, but he didn't want to be impolite, particularly as Cecil had a full packet of baccy in his hands, "No. Why?"

"They've got engaged."

Gurn stopped watching the preparation for the race and turned to the other two, "You realise what this means?"

The others shook their heads.

"This, my friends, is the beginning of the end."

*****

Printed in Great
Britain
by Amazon